WHAT REVIEWERS ARE SAYING...

ABOUT MAGGIE AWARD OF EXCELLENCE FINALIST, *ENSNARED BY INNOCENCE*:

"Witty, Enchanting and Roaring Hot!
I think I've found a new author to binge! I would definitely recommend it as a good gateway book to shape-shifters or to lovers of historical romance."
5-Star Goodreads Review

"I would give this a 10/10 rating. Beautifully written by a very talented author... PLEASE read this brilliant novel. I cannot wait for the next in series." 5-Star BookBub Review

"Oh. My. Goodness! This story caught my attention from page one. It is a fresh take on the shifter genre. **This Regency novel had every element a girl could want: several mysteries to solve, smokin' hot heroes and sensible, funny and courageous heroines.**" 5-star Goodreads review

"**Without a doubt, this author is going to the top of my favorite historical novel author list. I really loved this twist on the traditional historical romance novel.**" 5-star Goodreads review

"**Fantastic Story!!** I really enjoyed this book!" 5-Star Reviewer Emily P.

"I love the fact this is **shifter and regency** all rolled into one...I was amazed by the storyline and couldn't help how addictive I found this text...**I loved the originality of this book** and thought it really stood out for many reasons... **A true talent for writing...**" 5-Star Review

For the magical Jackie Rose, whose gift of enlightening others—to see both what is and what could be— knows no bounds. She's priceless, as are her teachings.

authorized, purchased downloads. All characters are fictional creations; any resemblance to actual persons is unintentional and coincidental.

Proofread by Judy Zweifel at Judy's Proofreading. Cover by Literary Madness.

At Literary Madness, our goal is to create a book free of typos. If you notice anything amiss, please let us know. litmadness@yahoo.com

CONTENTS

A FROSTY CHRISTMAS KISS

A WARM AND WITTY WINTER REGENCY

LARISSA LYONS

Perfect happiness, even in memory, is not common.

— JANE AUSTEN, *EMMA*

1

WHEN "FESTIVE" FEELS NIGH ON IMPOSSIBLE

THE SPECTER GAZED down from her perch betwixt cloud and atmosphere. For nigh on four years she'd been ready to join her precious babes on the other side but ere she crossed the final veil, she had her darling full-grown daughter to see properly cherished first. Not an easy task when her dearest Issybelle wasn't allowed off the estate. When the man who'd sired her daughter had become more jailer than father.

With a shake of her head, a flap of her angelic wings, she tossed off the troublesome thoughts. The season of miracles drew near. Was she not in the *proper place to orchestrate one of her own? Mayhap several?*

DECEMBER 25TH, 1813 ~ THE FIRST DAY OF CHRISTMAS

"PRAY, Anne, who is that fearsome fellow darkening your doorstep? Tut-tut. Such a tardy arrival."

"The black-haired frowning one, you mean?"

Isabella's ears perked up, awaiting the answer.

As Isabella Spier had no chance of seeing him for herself—being completely blind and in the dark as it were—she paid particular attention to the whispered comments.

Ensconced in her favored chair near the fireplace heating the great drawing room of her friend's home, inhaling the fragrant greenery the servants refreshed that very morning, and listening to the uplifting music —from the quartet commissioned for the entire twelve days—she'd never been more at peace.

Pure sunshine on a dank and dismal day— that's what Anne's company and home had been these past weeks.

Learning that the Spierton housekeeper, *un*affectionately known as The Warden, would be spending the winter with her family in Wales, Anne had presented her pregnant self at Spierton the first week in December and insisted on bringing Isabella to Redford Manor for the entire holiday "Starting today, which will give you time to learn the arrangement of the house and grounds at your leisure before anyone else arrives".

How the lure of a month of freedom from the fortress she called home had beckoned.

Her father was in London until after the new year. That, combined with Anne's monetary mischief, had sweetened the pot nearly beyond bearing.

Isabella had laughed when she'd learned of the gold coins that had changed palms. "You bribed our servants to not tattle?" she'd accused without rancor, deeply touched that merely the possibility of her company could inspire such devotion and generosity.

"Not bribes," Anne assured, "*bonuses*. Holiday bonuses. Something I'm sure your miserly father no doubt overlooks."

Eventually, with a lilt of joy in her heart, Isabella had succumbed to Anne's urging. She could do no less when Anne had added, "Come now, Issybee, he forbade your presence at our wedding. Would you deny me now too?"

Of course she couldn't, not now that circumstances had seen fit to provide a reprieve from her solitary station. What was the worst Father could do to Isabella upon discovering she'd dared leave without his permission? Banish her to an asylum? A convent? It wasn't as though he hadn't already applied those threats.

Though Mama was no longer around to grace Isabella with her shielding presence, neither was Isabella a child to be ordered about or threatened into obedience.

And after reminding herself of that three hundred times or more in the days that followed, she'd finally begun believing it, her life since The Disastrous Accident seeming more remote with every second that passed. With every delightful moment she spent surrounded by cheerful friends and carefree fellowship.

"Likely he's all Friday-faced because he missed receiving any gifts this morn." While she'd been woolgathering, speculation over the newcomer's identity had continued.

"Do tell, Anne," another lively voice chimed in, "who is he? I certainly wouldn't want to be seated next to such a glowering crank at dinner."

Amidst the excitement surrounding the grim arrival, the not-quite woman at her side leaned over and spoke in Isabella's ear. "To be sure, I find him rather handsome—always have—and if I were permitted to join the adults for dinner, you can be assured *I* would sit next to him. Or directly upon his lap."

Laughing at Harriet's emphatic pronouncement, Isabella missed the name of the belated guest. "Harriet!" she admonished Anne's younger sister with a smile. "Let Anne or your mother overhear you and it'll be straight to bed without any supper."

"That threat won't work. Miss Primrose would bring me biscuits and milk, I am sure." Harriet mentioned her governess, a soft-spoken woman who had earned Isabella's respect, given how she handled the energetic and outspoken Harri.

"Oh no she wouldn't," said the governess from Harriet's other side, likely tucked away in the nearest corner, ready to whisk the girl off at her mother's command. "You best be minding your manners, lest your evening with the adults be cut shorter than you might wish."

"Yes, ma'am," Harriet responded. But even that was offered with a hint of good-natured rebellion in her tone. "My manners shall be minded without further ado."

Nearing the "advanced" age of fifteen—which she continually liked to remind everyone—Harriet had appointed herself Isabella's guide upon her arrival, saying she was better suited to the task than Anne, not having a house full of guests to prepare for, and *not* being pregnant—which caused their mama to exclaim, "Thank the heavens for small favors! And don't you be getting any ideas, young lady."

Isabella soon became acquainted with the immense estate her friend had moved to upon her marriage to Lord Redford—or Edward, as he gave her leave to call him—and *reac-quainted* with Harriet whom she'd last visited with at such length almost ten years before when Harriet's only topic of conversation—

unlike her current fascination with men—tended to be that of kittens and kittens and more kittens.

A time when Isabella had still been in a position to *see*. Cats and ribbons and most everything else...

"A girl can dream, can she not?" Harriet sighed wistfully before straightening and rejoining the general conversation, leaving Isabella to ponder her own dreams for the remaining fortnight. A mere twelve days and the most wondrous holiday season she could imagine would be at its end, as would her expectation of ever enjoying anything so grand again.

But she refused to think of that now. Certainly not. Not with so many entertaining companions huddled nearby.

———— ⊃●⊂ ————

HE HADN'T WANTED to lend his presence. Hadn't wanted to dance and make bloody merry. Most especially, he hadn't wanted to celebrate the blasted Christmas Season.

Yet here he was.

Tidings be damned, he should've cried off.

He'd tried. Had, in fact, tendered every excuse he could legitimately think of—and a few illegitimate ones as well—but Ed would have none of it.

"It's Christmastime we're talking about," his longtime friend had proclaimed a month ago with all the persistence of a nagging nanny, as though Frost were still in the nursery instead of just acquiring a tidy sum over the pugilistic endeavors the two had wagered upon. "You simply *must* celebrate with us. I am not at liberty to brook refusal."

"You weren't this tenacious last year," Frost remarked dryly after his fifth excuse was shot down.

On foot, they headed to No. 23 Henrietta Street where Frost had offered to treat them both to the best beefsteak and ale around.

Perhaps the sustenance would lend strength to his arguments.

"Ah...but last year, our first as a married couple," Ed responded with an odd softening in his gaze—one Frost found unaccountably difficult to witness, "we celebrated the season with her parents, at the Larchmont home. *This* year, Anne insists we host you all at Redford Manor."

Then again, perhaps sustenance wouldn't aid his cause because beholding Ed's love for his wife was downright painful.

When had Frost ever felt *soft* toward another human being? Toward *anything* during the season under discussion?

He looked away and hastened his pace. Offley's wasn't far now. "I don't see how my presence will signify one way or the other."

"It signifies, and you know it. With all we've shared. Suffered together, how can you question that?"

"Suffered? *Me?*" Frost spared a glance at Ed's overly serious mien. "You're the one missing parts. Warrick's the one rolling about. I didn't lose one arm and crumble another. Lose the use of both legs—"

"Nicholas."

That was it, just his name. His *given* name.

Followed by a heavy sigh as Ed matched him stride for stride. "Yet you have been there every step—pardon the pun—of the way. Suffering right along with us, perhaps more—in your own way. Some wounds aren't visible, you know."

How he did know.

He ground his teeth, refusing to succumb

to the guilt hovering on the fringes, and waited. He knew there'd be more.

And he was right. "Beyond the war, it signifies because you're my friend, and now that your remaining family has passed on"—Ed glossed over the demise of Frost's contentious mother nearly a year past—"I don't want you spending the holiday alone."

Frost swallowed the instinctive retort. Though he counted Ed Redford among his most intimate of companions, had ever since the two of them shared rooms while at Oxford, he'd never divulged his apathy toward the holidays. Or the reasons behind it.

"Moreover," Ed continued, dodging the efforts of a Covent Garden nun to wave him down, "Anne charged me with the task of securing your attendance. She says we shall gather those closest to us and celebrate the spirit of the season with those we love."

At the reminder of the amiable, gregarious woman his friend had married, Frost finally allowed his jaw to unclench. "Might I ask why your paragon of a wife did not accompany you to tender this...this... Hmm, I'm not sure I would call such an impassioned appeal an *invitation*. A campaign, more like."

One with a well-thought-out battle plan, he acknowledged, feeling the familiar, holiday-induced irritation start to take hold. He ruthlessly shoved it away. December had yet to begin, and as they trudged through the dirty, wet streets of London, he was already smelling pine boughs and evergreen, however impossible, tasting gingerbread and wassail and bloody wanting to spit.

Simply the thought of the so-called "joyous season" soured his mood and his stomach. Maybe he'd skip the beefsteak for once, go straight to the ale.

"Quit demurring and I'll tell you." Ed's voice rang with happiness. "She's breeding, don't you know! I bid her to stay at home while I met with my solicitor and called on you. We suspected you'd likely disdain any written invitations, as you have our prior requests to join us."

"Disdain? I have done no such thing." But neither had he responded to the three separate missives.

"Ignore, then. Come now, I want you with us as well. Were it not for you, I may not have made it home for there to be a wedding. *Or at all.*" Granted, Frost had ridden in and rescued his fallen comrade at Albuera, before further damage could be done, after a blade from a French dragoon found its mark, knocking Ed from his horse and severing the lower part of one arm in a mangled slice that required full amputation, but he was uncomfortable with the reminder.

"You know I prefer to observe Christmastide here." *Alone.*

In actuality, he spent the days just as he did any other...if colder of heart and chillier of soul.

Seeing both his friends so severely injured —simply enduring his miserable mother in the years before that—had taught him one thing: avoidance. If one avoided feeling, one avoided hurting.

"Then it's time for a change, by damn. I'm sure it won't equal the level of revelry you're used to but be assured we'll try." Little did Ed know the traditions of Frost's youth, the ones he'd spent so much time at Oxford blathering on and on about, were nothing more than figments of a guilty imagination. He'd last celebrated a true Christmas when he was eleven, and he had no intention of ever doing so again. He despised the holidays and everything they stood for—family and merriment and memories.

God, how he detested the memories. The only way he could muster through the wretched season was if he faced it more soused than sober.

This is what came of attending Ed's betrothal kick-up two years prior—the mistaken impression that Frost *wanted* to racket about in society. Not hardly. Yet after all their side had suffered, had lost, in 1811, once both Redford and their friend Warrick mustered the will to overcome the physical mulligrubs caused by the blasted war, Frost's conscience had given him no choice. But now?

Avoidance bled loneliness, aye, but also a modicum of peace. "What of Warrick?" he thought to bargain. "Will his recreative presence not suffice?"

Compared to his unwilling company, Warrick's jovial bent would certainly foster more good cheer in those weak enough to yield to Ed's plaguey urgings.

For himself, Frost knew better than to surrender, his thoughts still too frequently mired not in merriment, but back in time, on the battlefield...

. . .

PICKING through the bodies littered upon the soggy ground, hours after the fighting halted, searching for any improbable survivors. Searching more specifically for Warrick, who hadn't gathered with the rest of them when the order had gone out.

Pausing to retch—the sights and stench turning his stomach and churning his heart until nothing but a hollow shell remained. Brittle and broken.

A whimper, weak and breathy, but miraculously sighing *his* name met his straining ears over the remembered sounds of the earlier battle, the shouts and weapon fire competing with the hail and rain storming down on them as though the Almighty himself had disapproved of the fight being waged.

Frost stilled, drew in a deep breath after wiping his mouth free of spittle. "Warrick!"

Nothing, blast it.

Nothing beyond the wind, carrying the scents of death and despair. Nothing but his conscience waging its own war with duty. Why had he not returned home by now? With his father's demise some years hence, and the full weight and responsibility of the title and estates now entrenched on his broad and battered shoulders...

"Warrick!" Had he imagined the earlier sound? "You damn reprobate! Where the hell are you?"

"Saint Nick..."

Blessed saints, it came again—the nickery he'd been saddled with by his school chums. He lurched to his feet. Started plundering through yet another heap of bodies until he found the one he sought.

That's when the real work began... Extricating an insensible fifteen-stone comrade who had lost the ability to move.

Anything but his tongue, it seemed.

"I say, naggin' Nicky-boy," Warrick slurred, while Frost frantically dug past the dead covering his fallen mate, needing to search beneath his friend's filthy uniform, locate the injury that had assailed him. "Angels, I tell you. Flappin' those glitt'ry wings..."

Warrick was still muttering, jawing about as though he had something to say, and for once, his blather was the most welcome sound Frost could imagine. "...the hopes of carting me off. Till you got your muddy hands on my digs."

"Angels? Pah." Frost heaved another dead soldier—a Frog, this time—from Warrick, nearly casting up his accounts again, nothing left but bile, when half the man's innards fell out. Biting his lips, his cheeks puffed against the urge to cascade, he shuddered. Suffered through more nonsensical jabber while he brought his stomach under control.

"Apple-fed pigs would be more likely to cart off your burdensome carcass," he told Warrick. "Pray to your angels, man. I need some aid."

Frost dropped to his knees, inspecting Warrick's muck-covered torso and legs, fighting against his friend when Warrick persisted in twisting his shoulders, arms reaching upward, to some unseen sight far beyond Frost's fathom, before his mate groaned, grimaced in pain or sorrow, tears leaking from the edges of his eyes even as he cursed like the devil, sinking back into the muddy ground.

"Blazes, Nick..." Warrick wound down his vocal tirade, using the name from their school days, instead of the formal *Lord Frost-wood* he'd been harrying him with in recent years. "Can see naught but you getting pert with my groin and pizzle. I don't conjobble that way, man. Or are you tryin' to help me piss? God *damn*—'pologies, angels—but I can't feel—"

"Help me, damn you," Frost grunted, winded by the effort of gaining Warrick to his feet, after confirming nothing was falling out of *his* middle. Worried about both his friends. Worn beyond frazzled by the blasted war. "Got to get you back up on my horse, for I have no hope of carrying your heavy arse—"

"Not t'day, you crank of a commandin' officer. Angels said I could fly with them. *Fly*, man. Or wait. For you. Your tardy hide. No walkin' today. Maybe never." A deep moan ruptured up from Warrick then, the pain slicing through Frost despite his efforts to stay enured, to blunt back all the human misery his job and evil Bonaparte caused.

More groans. More insensible angelic mutterings. More blood and tears (these, his own, hidden by the sweat, thank the God Frost had begun to doubt more and more of late). Until finally, he delivered a now-unconscious Warrick to the field doc who only shook his head and ordered Warrick's body be dumped in a pile with his lost patients. Those either gone. Or nearly so.

The row that followed should have at least brought down a few of Warrick's angels. It was certainly loud enough to summon them. But the colorful content spewing between the two men—one a determined officer and stalwart friend; the other a ravaged, overworked and heartsick physician—was more suited to summoning demons.

In the end, Frost had his way, the doctor had his say: "He won't thank you. Won't walk again, not with these injuries. Likely going to wish you'd left him back there. Let him expire in peace."

Peace? In pieces, more like, given the reavers coming to scour the battlefield, taking anything and everything off the deceased and dying. Heaven's angels would come down and whisk Frostwood off—not likely—before he would let that happen.

He inhaled, ready to rail at the physician all over again, when a new voice surprised them both—

"No, he won't." Bloody bandage wrapped around his mostly severed arm, waiting for the accommodating doc here to finish the job, forehead pale, eyes glassy and cheeks flushed with pain, Ed Redford had made his way inside unnoticed and spoke from his perch on a cot in the corner. "Warrick is too glib for hell, and I'm not sure he's earned his way to heaven yet." Damn, but Ed's voice was weak. "He'll fight. Feet or no. Legs or not." Ed gave a nod to his hanging-by-skin-and-ligaments arm. "Least he'll have them, even if they don't work."

And with that, the sawbones got back to the nasty business of just that—sawing bones. Frost loaded Warrick onto the cart of survivors too injured to walk. And he kept Warrick's angel ramblings to himself.

For even if his friend *had* earned his way upstairs, who would believe him?

"NOTHING on the grand scale you enjoyed growing up..."

Ed was still talking?

It took a moment for Frost to bring his mind back from the painful past and into the present.

"Ours is simply a little gathering of friends and family, and we want you with us. Come now—"

"And Warrick?" Frost interrupted, still working to rid himself of the muddle and memories of Spain. "Is he gracing us with his convivial presence this year? Ready to wheel about the ballroom floor with the latest Diamond?"

At least if Warrick was there, the ladies would be all over his Merlin's-chair-bound hide. Because while the pain of war may have stolen his mobility, Warrick's mouth still worked fine. And unmarried females, or so Frost had observed, felt an enviable ease flirting with a man confined to a wheeled chair and were wont to leave Frostwood alone. Just the way he preferred it.

"You're not attending my discourse—and after you inquired." Ed stopped walking and spun to clasp his hand around Frost's upper arm—with an impressively firm grip, a pronounced improvement over the broken bones and misshapen mess his remaining hand had been two and a half years ago. "Did you not hear me earlier? That newfangled doctor his mother found last year? There's something to his unorthodox methods. Warrick is actually his wiggling toes now! Declined our invitation because he didn't want to halt any potential progress. He's spending extra time with his physician over the holidays. Anne and I are catching up with him after the New Year, going to travel before she's too big to fit in the carriage."

Frost chuckled at the jest as he was meant to.

It was better than making a bad-mannered comment about wiggling toes. If he decamped a boot and wiggled his, would Ed let him remain in London?

"Saint Nick"—oh, that was low, calling forth well over a decade of friendship now?—"how can you deny Anne's request when it is one I myself echo a thousand times over?"

How indeed?

"Aye, I'll be there," Frost finally conceded just as they reached their destination, anticipating the ale more than ever.

Envisioning all the holiday larking he'd just agreed to, thoughts of the sugary, sickening wassail he and his sister had loved sneaking sips of as children nearly strangled him. He needed to drown the recent memories of bile and stench every bit as much as the older ones of cider and spices that now coated his tongue.

"Be forewarned, I do have other invitations." Which was true, although he'd declined every single one with no hesitation whatsoever. "Other commitments. So I'll likely not arrive until the eve of Christmas or the morning of and don't expect me to stay the full twelve days."

"Aww, Nick—"

"Or I could not come at all," he added coldly, wondering when he'd started living up to the appellation *Frigid Frost*, assigned by his former mistress directly after she bid him *adieu* with a flying porcelain figure—straight to his head. Decapitated the poor flute-playing shepherd with his hard rock of a noggin, he had, splitting his eyebrow open in the process.

"Your brusque ways hold no sway with me, old friend. You said you'd be there, ergo, I'll tell Anne to expect you."

So it was with ill-disguised dread that Nicholas Michael Henry Winten, seventh Earl of Frostwood and despiser of everything merry, made his way downstairs for the evening's entertainments, having arrived as late as he dared at Redford Manor.

The first of twelve supposedly festive nights he'd be forced to endure before departing on the celebrated day of Epiphany, January 6th. *Unless* he decided to retreat earlier...

"Thunderation!" he muttered beneath his breath, pounding down the ribbon-and-ivy-bedecked stairs. How he abhorred Christmastime.

2

THE FESTIVITIES BEGIN...
AND A CERTAIN FROSTY
FELLOW IS BLIND TO THE
TRUTH

———◦◦———

HOW SHE ADORED CHRISTMASTIME.

The sounds, the scents, the very feel in the air that fostered such a beautiful sense of exuberance and harmony.

Isabella let the warmth from the fire soothe the chill in the air and the companionship soothe the one in her bones, finally losing the apprehension that had gripped her during the first days of her visit. The anxiousness that spiked once the guests began arriving and she'd feared tripping over someone, being in the way and generally making a nuisance of herself.

She'd been relieved to discover her fears were all for naught as her first weeks at Redford Manor passed without mishap. She really had been imprisoned at Spierton, Isabella was dismayed to realize. Anne had claimed it was so, ever since Isabella's mama went to her heavenly rewards four years ago and Isabella's father neglected to do the same—or so Anne accused, saying if he had any consideration for his sole progeny at all, he would've been generous enough to depart for his own *hellish* rewards.

Isabella could snicker over the thought now, after time away from his overbearing presence. But with no dowry (Father refused to spend a cent of his blunt "advertising a defective wife likely to breed defective heirs") and no chance of receiving callers (he generally turned visitors away before they reached the gate), Isabella had long since faced the certainty of her situation. She had no hope of marriage and little hope of a happy ending to match her friend's.

"Ooo, look yonder, comin' in from the card room, a veritable bonny tulip among men, that waistcoat is surely the brightest shade of green and yellow paisley I ever did see." a Scottish

neighbor complimented Lord Redford's visiting cousin Aylmer. 'Twas not the first time his
appearance had garnered comments.

"Wears his inexpressibles too tight if you
take my meaning," Anne's mother huffed,
causing Isabella to free a smile. Who needed
their own good fortune when they could share
in others'?

"Did you notice precisely where the fabric's
come undone?" Harriet asked everyone in a
loud whisper. "Between his legs...high on the
inside of his left thigh?"

"Harriet! Be gone with you, girl, if you're so
impudent as to mention such a thing."

Isabella's smile widened.

"That spot is practically at eye level, Mama,
when one is seated as we are. I even believe I
can see two hairs peeking—"

Anne gasped to cover a giggle. Her mother
squawked and two more women made
swooning noises while the rest of them, Isabella included, only laughed out loud.

"I cannot help but notice," Harriet
protested sincerely. "They are right *there*."

"Up! Up with you, young lady, and straight
to bed!"

Isabella made every attempt to subdue her

mirth but failed miserably. Poor Harriet, she didn't even have the promise of a new kitten to soften the scold that would likely be ringing in her ears the remainder of the night.

Isabella did a quick calculation. Including the frowning newcomer, most all of the anticipated party had arrived. There were to be eighty-eight guests and she'd met eighty or eighty-one...having lost the exact count somewhere between Lady Fairfax and her daughter —Or was it daughters?—and the Gregory brothers, two gentlemen who both flattered Isabella with Spanish coin until she knew her face must be as red as the satin ribbons Anne told her graced every available surface.

What had Miss Fairfax's name been? Uriana? Or was it Amelia? A blighted fly upon her brain for not remembering. Either way, the unfortunate girl had a dreadful case of snuffles.

"Lady Isabella," a precise, clipped voice interrupted the feminine chatter, addressing her directly, "may I have the honor of escorting you to dinner?"

As if conjured by her thoughts, it was one of the Gregory brothers, though she hadn't made sufficient distinction between them to know which. Concentrating on holding her gaze steady as she and Mama had practiced, Isabella focused on the speaker. "You may indeed, kind sir."

She rose and, with her steps lighter and more sure than she'd expected weeks ago, made her way from the room on his arm.

———————◦◦◦———————

DINNER WAS A BORE. Everyone in attendance was a bore.

Hell, *he* was the bore, Frost realized, noticing the downward turn of his thoughts and forcing his lips into a smile. It felt like a grimace so he tried again, ordering his lips and cheeks to cooperate. He was here after all, he could at least attempt to do the pretty, to act the gentleman.

He'd been told he had adorable dimples, might as well release them for the holiday. His gift, as it were.

Adorable, blast and damn, the bane of every male. As a youth, he'd undergone significant practice to eradicate the dreaded indentations, and by the time he needed to scrape whiskers off his jaw, he'd ruthlessly taught himself how to suppress any hint of a damn dimple, adorable or otherwise.

Draining his wineglass for the seventh time—a number that tended to grow each year around this particular date—he resolved to ask at least one of the unmarried females to dance that evening. He could do that, could he not—mask his irritation for a single dance during the night's promised entertainment? Surely he could, he thought with a smile that likely belonged on a hyena. So long as it wasn't a bloody *Christmas* song.

———◦———

Nicholas Winten, Earl of Frostwood...a chilly nomenclature for such a fiery fellow. Cold and unfeeling he might be perceived, but she saw beneath exteriors. Always had—since the day she lost hers.

Anger and resentment simmered below his frosty façade. That and a cartload of hurt. Poor chap, he was taking after his termagant of a mother —the most unpleasant creature to dash across her path in the ether, heading south if the disagreeable cackle and hateful remarks were anything to go by.

But she could sense how his moods were

nothing more than contrivances to protect the wounded boy hiding inside. A little boy she suspected Issybelle would know just how to reach—and heal.

———————◦○◦———————

THE DANGLING RINGLET upon Isabella's forehead swayed with the motion of her feet. She'd requested the maid arrange it just so, and every light brush was a reminder of how pleasing it was to have her wishes regarded.

Spine flush against the wall, Isabella's toes rose and fell in time with the lively music. Her right hand, snug upon the strap of her fan, tapped against her thigh in tandem with her dancing toes. She itched to be alone. To indulge in her one vulgar pastime—or so Father labeled it, saying the habit made her look no better than a "bingo mort", a female drunkard —the activity that had earned her more than one bruised shin and worse, Father's further disdain. But all the same, the obsession beckoned.

But it was not to be. Not now that the other guests had arrived and she no longer had the privilege of finding herself *alone* in the great ballroom.

The beginnings of the third set reached her ears. Everyone not already breathless with exertion rushed onto the dance floor at Anne's prompting. As mistress of the assembly, Anne presided over the dances and called the steps, just as they'd played and practiced when they were younger. Her friend's happiness was evident.

More than ever, Isabella yearned to join in.

"Dance with me."

Her head jerked toward the speaker. Startled by the abrupt command, as well as by the rich voice that pronounced it, she blinked. Was he talking to her? Or someone else nearby?

Anne had dispensed with the custom of dance cards, instructing her guests to mingle and make merry as they saw fit. This wouldn't be the first man to take pity on her and offer to escort her around the floor. But he would be the first to do so without at least introducing himself or extending a greeting.

"Pardon?" Isabella inquired softly, testing her perception.

He shifted closer. She felt his presence

fairly sizzle along her front. "I said, 'Dance with me'."

"That is what I thought you said. Well, sir..." Isabella began with true regret, for she longed to dance and for some odd reason given his inexcusable curtness, she especially longed to dance with the owner of the velvet-voiced commands. She certainly hadn't entertained such longing when declining the four previous, *courteous* offers she'd received, but then each of those men had been known to her. "I fear I must decline your less-than-polite dictum."

In direct contrast to his abrupt tone, she gave a gracious nod then turned toward the open doors she knew to be on her left, running her corresponding hand lightly along the wall.

"*What*?" he snapped the same instant she felt his fingers encircle her opposite wrist, halting her progress. "You reject me?"

Had not her fan been affixed to her arm she surely would've dropped it at the unexpected touch—and her reaction to it.

"Reject you? Nay," she said, trying to dismiss the nuance of hurt she detected in his haughty voice. Just as she tried to dismiss how the fingers above her glove seared her skin.

Had she ever felt the touch of a man not family on her flesh before? Why certainly she had... Physicians for one—

Shaking herself free of his hold and her own disturbing thoughts, Isabella reiterated, "Nay, but I *do* reject your tone for I dislike intently being ordered about."

"Ah...then it is I who must beg your pardon," he said smoothly—too smoothly. It was a rakeshame she had the misfortune to be bantering with, Isabella feared, feeling how the subtle shift in his demeanor caused her insides to riot. "For though I have been returned from war these two years past, I fear old habits of barking commands have yet to leave my lips. *Would* you perchance care to dance? *Perchance to dance?*" he self-mocked. "From commander to pitiful poet, I fear. I only ask because you..."

"I...what?"

"You..."

Why was he still hesitating? Though his unexpected humor distracted her mightily, she heard plainly what he refused to voice. So she said it for him. "I am the only pitiable female not yet engaged?"

"No! You...you have a curl in your eye," he

accused as though she'd committed a crime and the pillory awaited.

"Mayhap I like it there."

"Well, I do not."

Subduing the urge to twitch her head and dislodge the curl he somehow found so offensive, Isabella wondered why, if she irritated him so, he remained. And why, a foxed pox on her sudden boldness, was conversing with him exhilarating beyond belief?

This daring side she'd released was wont to land her in trouble.

Thanks to her father, she'd learned early and well to hide her love of music and movement. A lesson she'd best not allow a domineering stranger tempt her into forgetting. "Well, sir, as much as I like my curl's present location, mayhap I wish *you* gone."

She thought he sputtered a protest but didn't give her ears time to decide. "Because I most certainly do *not* care to dance, especially not with you," she lied, for she irrationally wished it above all things. "Good evening, sir."

Quickly, she quit the room before he could —shameless rake or gruff commander, she knew not which—blast through her common sense and have her agreeing. To *dance* with him of all things.

I AM the only pitiable female not yet engaged?

Damn and blast! That wasn't what he'd been about to say. Not even close.

You have a curl in your eye.

Blast and damn, that wasn't what he'd meant to say either. She muddled his tongue, this obstinate, enchanting miss.

An uncommon beauty, at least to him, Frost thought now, recalling her wistful expression as she held up one side of the ballroom. A lone, confident figure who invited and intrigued...

I only ask because you stare so longingly at the dance floor...with just a hint of sorrow. I thought perhaps you were reliving an earlier time and we might banish our memories together, if only for a song.

But he hadn't been able to bring himself to utter such romantic drivel.

The lack of courage had cost him. Cost the acquaintance of the most promising miss present and there certainly wasn't a lack, Ed and Lady Redford having invited half the shire from what he could tell. "Little gathering for the holidays" indeed. Had to be close to ninety revelers in his estimation. Might as well have been five hundred for all the maggoty "cheer" such a crush harkened upon his person.

Hell, he'd only promised himself a single dance as a singular act of charity, little expecting to be captivated and then outright rebuffed, but that's exactly what happened. Perhaps the saucy baggage did it on purpose, to snare his interest.

Intentionally or not, she'd succeeded, for though her head was topped with sable brown ringlets instead of ones reminiscent of corn silk, with that primly spoken refusal—not to mention the dreadfully alluring curl—the impudent wench who dared defy him tonight not only tripped up his tongue, she put him in mind of the last female *he'd* dared to love, harking him back nearly two decades to the oft-heard complaint of another...

"Nicky, you cannot order me about like one of your soldiers," his sister Althea had insisted in a familiar refrain. "I will not stand for it!"

"There's—" He'd broken off, coughing over his shoulder, that niggling tickle that'd scratched his throat for weeks coming to the fore. When it subsided, he tweaked one of the gold ringlets that was forever falling over her eye. "There's a fierce puss."

She tossed her head, slinging ringlets straight into his face.

He'd laughed at her eight-year-old antics —*so* much younger than his own mature eleven—and pointed to the battalion on the floor between them. An entire regiment of new toy soldiers given to him by Papa for Christmas. "Now set up the right flank for the next offensive lest I tell Mama how you tore your dress."

Following him out to the stables that morning was how. But he never had an opportunity to snitch, for in the night, Althea came down with his cough. And breathed her last less than a fortnight later...

Staggered by the unexpected memory— though during the recollection of it, his disobedient lips had curved upward—Frost firmed his frown.

Without conscious thought, his right hand coiled into a fist...the same hand that had gripped *her* yet had been unable to prevent her escape. The same hand that warmed oddly for such an innocent, brief touch.

Damn and blast all over again. He'd not expected to *react* to a female here of all places —and at this time of year? What else he hadn't expected was having his overture rebuffed. Shot down like an unwitting bird in the sky. First his excuses, now *his* invitation. "Good thing I didn't have this kind of luck in front of the French artillery."

"What kind of luck?" Ed wanted to know, coming up beside him with a fancy kissing bough hanging from his truncated arm.

"Nothing," Frost dismissed then nodded to the berry-filled bough. "Be so good as to inform me where you intend to hang that thing so I may avoid its reach."

Ed grinned. "'Tis one of many, my friend, so it will do you no good to cast this one into the fire as that scowl tells me you're wont to do the moment my back is turned. Anne has ordered them strewn about the place. Says I'm to make full use of them but only when *she's* in reach."

The bountiful look in Ed's eyes—his friend healed, if not quite whole—thanks in part to his lovely wife? Painful. Like a knife to Frost's heart, the sheer happiness shining from Ed beamed forth like warm rays of sunshine that cut Frost to his cold-hearted core.

"She's had me hanging them the past half hour. Down to my last one."

"Have you not servants for that sort of task?"

"And miss the enjoyment of surprising her when she learns just how creative my hanging places can be?"

Frost stifled a yawn that was only partially faked. The trip from London had been a tiring one, and of course he'd waited until the last moment to make it, arriving only minutes before dinner. Then imbibing rather too freely during...

"I'm sure tomorrow will come early and be full of merriment," he somehow managed to say without choking on the last word, his eyes drawn to the door she'd flown through. "Think I'll make a night of it."

Ed laughed. "You don't know the half. Anne has a seeking game planned if the weather proves cooperative. She's partnered you with—"

"Spare me tonight." Frost held up a hand, finding the thought of any organized holiday game nauseating. Or maybe it was the cloying scents of pine and fir that were making him nauseous. That or an impertinent curl. "Damn ballroom smells like a forest," he grumbled. "Not another word about it, Ed. I'll deal with tomorrow on the morrow. Make my excuses to your dear wife. I promise I'll be better company after a full night's rest."

Hieing off to his room and to bed should have been accomplished in a trice, but Frost was restive. Or so he told himself when instead of heading toward the guest wing where his assigned chamber awaited, he turned in the opposite direction...exploring. *Searching.*

His cheeks felt peculiar. He reached up to touch one, and that's when Frost realized he was smiling. Smiling at the audacity of the fresh-faced chit who had left him standing there, rejected.

By Zeus, he finally decides to do his duty and ask a wench to dance and the only one he approaches shows him her backbone in denying him, and then her backside—alluringly curved, he couldn't help but notice—as she walks away.

Amazing. Both that she turned him down and that he found it humorous.

"Insane." He checked Ed's study and the

library, declined refreshment when a servant passing in the hall offered such, made quick work investigating the balcony along the second floor, as well as two smaller parlors he chanced across, looked in the drawing room where they'd gathered before dinner, the card room—which was much attended at the moment—and the billiard room.

Though he must've encountered every damn guest *not* on the dance floor and avoided seven of Ed's blasted kissing boughs, he didn't catch sight nor sound of the woman he sought.

Where the devil had she gone off to and why the devil did he care?

It wasn't as though untidy brown ringlets and annoying, green-as-holly, unusually pale peepers were anything worth obsessing over. Neither was her trim figure sheathed in flowing lavender or her pinkened cheeks. An attractive, wholesome package to be sure, but nothing he hadn't seen a hundred times over.

Yet obsess he did.

Over that obstinate mouth he craved to taste—almost as much as he craved hearing it spout unexpected retorts.

Breathing deeply after ascending yet another set of stairs—of thinking of her mouth?

—Frost consciously subdued his efforts and the sense of inexplicable anticipation surging through him.

He had eleven more days to learn who she was. To convince her to dance with him. To forget why he hated Christmas and wasn't supposed to be feeling something as unexceptional as *excitement* over spending it here. With *her*.

The unnamed nobody he'd yet to garner an introduction to.

The woman who caused him to remember his past with something *other* than pain.

3

A FESTIVE SEARCH

━━━━━◆◦◆━━━━━

ISABELLA STOOD beside the open front door, cold air blasting her exposed cheek, telling herself not to be anxious. She trusted Anne, who'd assured her several times over that Isabella could fully participate in the day's activities.

The great hall was filled with scarf-and-mitten-bedecked females, with hatted and multi-caped coated gentlemen. Or so Harriet had described before departing to inspect Aylmer's pantaloons "On the chance today's have any holes in peculiar places too".

Though she wore the requisite bonnet and

scarf, Isabella had slipped her unmittened hands into the beautiful white ermine muff Anne had given her for Christmas (both Anne and Harriet had described the gift, but their words hadn't been necessary—its exquisite texture was sufficient to conjure hazy images in her mind). Feeling the anticipation as much as any other guest yet unable to move about on her own, Isabella repeatedly instructed her restless fingers to stop twitching within the confines of the sumptuous fur.

Really...she had no cause for being at sixes and sevens, having committed to memory the number of steps needed to exit the great hall and descend the stairs where the carriages would be waiting to convey them into town—the alluded to destination.

Unfortunately the knot of nervous dread in her stomach refused to cooperate, her anxiety deepening by the second. Of a certainty, her reaction couldn't have anything to do with hearing each doublet of names Anne called out, pairing the guests, and suspecting after name upon name was announced and mentally checking each off her list that she was about to be partnered with the brash stranger from last night.

The man whose identity she'd yet to learn or whose scent she'd not yet been successful in eradicating from her nostrils. Wretched nose. It remembered everything. The way he smelled richly of sandalwood, his breath of wine. The way—

"And that leaves us with our remaining duo..." Anne paused for effect. "Frost and Isabella!"

"Frost?" she whispered, testing the wintry name upon her tongue.

"Aye," his smooth voice responded from right in front of her.

Buffets of wind, amidst bustling and laughing and promises of more instructions once they reached town, battered Isabella from all sides as, now partnered, everyone deserted the hall in a mass exodus that barely granted Isabella enough time to mask her surprise before her left arm was tucked along his, her right being abandoned to fidget alone within the warm muff. Well now, she certainly hadn't planned very wisely for this occurrence.

"What? No gloves?" He made no attempt to hide his surprise.

Who needed them when a human brick burned beneath their hand? "I'm afraid I misplaced them," she admitted. "I searched every-where this morn, but my efforts proved futile for they weren't to be found."

He placed his leather-encased hand over her bare one, pressing her arm intimately against his side. "I expect they'll reveal them-selves when the maids see to your room."

"Yes, most likely."

"Shall we, then?" She heard the undercur-rent of laughter. "Note that I used inflection to indicate a question. But I do believe we should be off as we're lagging behind the others, being the last of the company to depart."

Stunned silent by his unexpected manner and her own silly schoolgirl response to it—to him—Isabella found herself clutching his arm and being guided down the front steps—eleven in all, she knew—without having time to utter more than a repetitive, "Frost?"

"Nicholas Winten, Earl of Frostwood," he confirmed just as their feet met the gravel driveway.

She hesitated, wondering why the impa-tient stomping of horses and jingle of har-nesses didn't greet her ears. His grip tightened but his pace didn't slow. Not a fraction. Nei-ther did her heart rate when he added, "I regret how our acquaintance started off with a bit of a contretemps last eve and I shall endeavor to rectify any less-than-perfect impression I may have left you with. I vow to make it up to you by being partner *par excellence* today at whatever brand of merriment our dear hostess has arranged. In exchange, you must tell me who you are—I only heard your given name—and agree to dance with me this evening."

His steps flew as fast and as sure as his words. She curved her hand tightly around his muscled forearm and tried to keep up. "Must I? If you continue to order me about, Lord Frostwood, I daresay I shall only continue to refuse everything you desire."

Oh heavens. Lord *Frostwood*?

Why had she not cobbled it together sooner? For upon saying the name, her mind conjured the picture painted for her last night —how Harriet had described the friend of Edward's when Isabella joined her after leaving the ballroom. The conversation she hadn't been able to put from her mind even after retiring...

"Posh. How that silly truffle Brighde thinks Cousin Aylmer is handsome when Lord Frostwood is in the room, I'll never know. I vow, he—"

"Frostwood?" Isabella had asked, latching on to the unfamiliar name.

"Oh yes! His countenance is divine, even when he's scowling. Shall I describe him to you? He has thick black curls and the darkest midnight eyes, and he's every bit as tall as Edward." That last part was no help at all, given how Isabella had never so much as touched Edward, much less sought to measure his height. "I vow, he must have his valet take a razor to his cheeks twice a day for there's always a hint of shadow after an hour or two. He has a strong nose. It quite puts me in mind of those old Roman busts in Papa's study. He was at the wedding, you know. Frost I mean, not any Roman emperors." Harriet laughed at her own wit.

"My..." Isabella could envision him so clearly it was disconcerting. She forced a casual observation. "My, but you have studied him, now haven't you?"

"Only because he and Lord Warrick are the most interesting of Ed's friends. They served together on the peninsula, did you know? Until Ed had to come home, that is. I vow, Lord Frostwood is so handsome I could swoon!"

The histrionics had continued into the night, as had the complaints she wasn't allowed to stay up and dance, descriptions of Cousin Aylmer's leg hair—still worthy of a laugh, though most improper—and the occasional detail about Lord Frostwood interspersed among her other diatribes.

Details Isabella drank up like parched earth and committed to memory.

"His papa died several years ago then his mother last spring...the deepest dimples adorn his cheeks—*if* one can catch him smiling...his skin is very bronze, as if he spends hours in the sun or is part gypsy. Would that not be something? Imagine if he were a gypsy! We could prevail upon him to foretell our futures..."

Dimples, rumors of his surly nature, descriptions of haughty, coal-black eyebrows— raised whenever his ire was piqued... Harriet waxed on and Isabella had provided a captive, if quiet audience.

At the thought of grazing her fingers over bristly whiskers...of searching out a hoarded dimple, Isabella stumbled.

His barked, "Have a care!" brought her

firmly into the present. Swoon-worthy dimples aside, there existed positively no reason for her to be intrigued by the reputedly cold, austere gentleman. Though his strong arm beneath her fingertips felt anything but cold...

Silly widgeon. Becoming all breathless over dimples you cannot even see. Or mayhap 'twas his accelerated pace. "Must you trod so quickly?"

"Quickly?" he asked in clear astonishment, making no effort to pause or shorten his stride. "Nay. Step lively now, for we have fallen behind every other pairing and do not want to lose ere we—"

"Ahhh!" Pain soared across her toes when her slippered foot met resistance. Tottering forward, she jerked her arm free and scrambled for balance.

Which she only found once she'd crashed to the ground. Her only thought—beyond what a wretched time to trip—was over her new muff. She'd lost it. "Dratted gnats."

"Isabella!" Anne cried in the distance.

He dropped to her side at once. She'd barely caught her breath, of a certainty considered her composure—along with her muff—still misplaced, when she felt large, *bare* hands begin combing every inch of her feet and legs. "Lord Frostwood," Isabella gasped. "Such liberties you—"

"Liberties? Blast it, woman," he said harshly, "you gave me a fright. Your legs, your ankles—"

"They are fine, my lord." She could even wiggle her toes now that the initial throbbing had dulled to an annoying ache. "But do you see—"

"You 'my lord' me *now*? Don't stand on ceremony, woman!" he snarled, taking one palm in hand, a palm she realized stung deeply. "You're bleeding. Are you injured elsewhere?"

"'Tis nothing more than a flea bite, certainly not worth all this fuss." She attempted to pull free and gain her feet, but he wouldn't have it.

"'Tis not a trifle. Both your palms are scraped raw. What else—"

"Isa...bella!" Sounding horribly out of breath, Anne reached them. "Frost...you imbecile! I paired you with Issybee...because I trusted you to look out for her. I trusted you!"

The hands holding hers strained with suppressed force. "*Imbecile*, Lady Redford?"

"Of course, you cork-brained simpleton! Can you not assist her—"

"Anne."

Edward's voice joined the fray and Isabella slumped toward Lord Frostwood, wanting to hide her face—if not her entire body. Her other palm burned too. Her legs and feet, save for one very tender toe, felt fine —if excessively tingly after being stroked by Lord Frostwood's warm-fingered hands. Had she not been so embarrassed by the fall, she'd be embarrassed by how her insides were now sweating at his proximity. None of the other men she'd met affected her thusly. Why him?

"Merry Anne." Edward spoke soothingly. "I don't think he realizes—"

"*Realizes*?" Anne screeched, and Isabella prayed no one else had joined them.

She straightened away from the surprising comfort of Lord Frostwood's impossibly hard chest and sought to smooth over any discomfort her clumsiness had caused—smoothing her skirts being out of the question as he still had command of her wrists. "I am fine, truly."

"Oh Isabella, dear—"

"'Tis nothing but a scratch." Lord Frostwood angled her hands. "Why the devil you go on—"

"A scratch!"

"Ed, tell your wife to quit harping at me, would you?"

"*Harping*?" Anne cried, her words shriller than the biting wind. "As if it isn't warranted! Could you not—"

"*Me*?" Lord Frostwood exploded. "Why is this about me, pray? Can the woman not watch where she's going?"

Sheer silence met his question.

Followed by two indrawn breaths—Anne's and Isabella's. He hadn't known?

Hadn't asked her to dance last night out of misplaced sympathy? Or flirted with her as a lark? Well now. How interesting.

But neither had he relinquished her hands, and Isabella was more than a little dismayed to realize she didn't want him to.

Anne recovered her surprise and spoke dryly. "Of course she could, Frost, if she could *see*. Isabella's blind, you imbecile."

"Blind?" The word was a growl. The hands surrounding hers tensed almost imperceptibly but she felt the subtle change nevertheless. Felt his strong hold skate along her arms, skitter over her legs, and somehow, flitter low about her belly. She was grateful for the new and distracting sensations; her embarrassment over falling in front of everyone paled to insignificance against the backdrop of his touch.

"Yes, blind," Edward confirmed. "As in her pretty glimms don't *see* you making an arse of yourself, old chap, but her wattles are working fine and can surely *hear* you being an arse. Speaking of which—Anne, I really must insist you stop calling my friend names."

"Not when I deserve them. Hel-*mmm*." He bit off the curse and shifted, releasing her at last. She stifled a mew of disappointment. Before she knew what he was about, he thrust one arm around her waist, the other beneath her legs, and hoisted her against his chest. Then he stood, bearing the entirety of her weight, without any apparent effort.

"I have you," he said with a silky tone she hadn't heard from him before at her instinctive squirm. She hadn't been held like this in...well, ever!

While her body acclimated to its new position, her lips protested. "This isn't nec—"

"It is." He cut her off, tightening his hold. "She twisted her ankle when she fell. I'll return to the house with her and see that she's cared for properly."

"But—"

He hefted her to hush the instinctive objection. "Ed, Lady Redford, you may be assured now that I am in possession of facts I lacked previously, I will be at great pains to ensure that Isabella comes to no further harm. Begone, both of you. See to your guests and their amusement. We shall find our own for the day."

Isabella opened her mouth to issue forth a complaint then thought better of it and snapped her lips shut. Scraped palms and smarting pride were a small price to pay for being carried in such strong arms, against such a broad chest and beneath such a tantalizingly scented neck. She inhaled and could swear her sore toe smiled in response.

Lord Frostwood's long, powerful strides carried her quickly away from familiarity and into the realm of wonder...of possibility. Smiling toes aside, her course was set after this idyllic, magical holiday. She knew that, had even managed to resign herself to her upcoming fate. So, what would be the harm in indulging in a bit of idle flirtation during the interim? *If* that was even something on his mind. But somehow she had a firm inkling that it was—and Isabella had long since learned to trust her senses.

Senses that clamored a moment later when she took stock of how fiercely her body responded to his nearness, jostled about with his forceful footsteps. She raised her right arm and stretched it over his head. Her fingers fluttered then found a perch above his collar... barely touching the strands of hair at his nape.

He hadn't said a single word. Not since capturing her person against his own as easily as he issued commands from that dimple-adorned mouth.

Isabella swallowed the knot of nervous excitement welling from her stomach to ask, "Why did you lie? Tell such a clanker about my ankle when I'd told you it was uninjured?"

WHY HAD HE LIED?

Because he felt the fool, the jester, the veriest of halfwits and needed to apologize and make amends, only he knew not how to begin.

Because she was fetching and fascinating

and it had been countless years since he'd been fascinated by anything.

Because when she was near, he felt anything but cold. The memories anything but painful.

"Because it was expedient," Frost informed her.

"Expedient?" she queried softly, and he fancied he felt her fingers caressing his neck.

"We need to have your injuries tended. This seemed the simplest way."

"Oh."

Blast. She sounded disappointed.

"And because I wanted you to myself for the day."

"Oh!"

———◆———

"ED? Should we let them return alone?" Anne questioned, concern prodding her conscience. "What if he—"

"Calm yourself. This is what you wanted to happen, is it not?"

"At the wedding. Not here—like *this*."

"These things happen in their own time. Let it be."

Ed pulled her around and added, "Nicholas is trustworthy, just...frosty."

"*Frosty?*" She left off gazing at the rapidly departing figure carrying her friend and skewered her mate with a glance full of righteous ire. "You jest? At a time such as this?"

"She shall come to no harm, that I can promise."

"She better not." Anne spied the ermine muff off to the side and bent to retrieve it. "Why did you not tell him? I cannot believe you—"

"Me? In case it escaped your awareness, we have other guests to attend." Indicating the churning clouds above, Ed took her arm and began guiding her reluctant form toward town. "We would all do well to enjoy our time outside before sleet chases us in. As to Frost and Isabella, I witnessed the two of them in conversation last eve and assumed you had already done so."

"I hadn't a chance, given how late he appeared, but..." Recalling how very protective Frost had been just now and the way Isabella had tucked herself against his chest, Anne allowed herself to relax. "It does appear that's of no consequence now. Forgive me. You are right

—I'm sure things between them will be fine as five pence in no time."

"Which is more than I can say for you if you insist on belittling my friends."

Anne heard his piqued tone and leaned into his side, brushing the silky fur over the stump of his missing arm. "I was worried about her, 'tis all."

"I know."

"I shall apologize to him."

Ed hugged her tight. "I know that too."

———◦———

A SATISFIED SMILE curved lips no longer human.

Nudging the maid tidying Isabella's room to put away the gloves had been inspired. Though perhaps not her best idea, given the condition of her daughter's hands. At least the act had necessitated Nicholas draw close to Issybelle—though it appeared he'd needed little prodding on that score.

A gentle wing fluttered behind her back in the nonexistent breeze. She brought its mate around and nestled her head within its softness, much as her daughter was doing against the man's neckcloth.

She watched him carrying her precious off-

spring and warmed at the sight, though she did wish she had someone to share her hope with. For now that Isabella had finally escaped the environs of her uncompromising father, there was much hope to be had.

Ah yes...skinned palms aside, a day well conceived.

4

A FESTIVE BERRY COMES TO HAND

———————◆———————

"Tell me how it happened."

Isabella considered reminding him not to order her about. But on some strange level she liked it—the way he paid her such focused attention. It was flattering after being all but ignored by her father for so long. And contrary to the sometimes smothering, sometimes doltish way—as if being blind somehow blinded her brain's ability to comprehend—strangers often prattled about in her presence, she rather liked how he treated *her* as she surmised he treated everyone else. In fact—

"Well?" his velvety voice intoned from far

above her position on the settee. Her posterior had barely connected with the upholstery before he barreled into the room, barking orders. "Prevaricate no more. We're alone now so have at it."

His obvious impatience made her smile. He'd given no quarter from the moment he'd set foot inside—still carrying her—quickly summoning a maid to put away their coats and scarves, and the housekeeper to clean, apply salve and bandage her palms. Noting how competently he made demands of servants who had no allegiance to him and even more, how quickly they complied with each of his wishes, caused her to realize what an imposing man she'd somehow collected as her champion.

Her entire left side came alive when he settled beside her and gingerly lifted each wrist, turning them hither and yon, scrutinizing the wrappings, or so she assumed when he complimented, "She is to be commended, that Mrs. Parksen. Did a fine job of it. How do they feel?"

Better now that he was holding them. "As though I dispatched my gloves, kicked my feet in the air and ran barehanded across the gravel path."

"Well, call me a cur's cracker!"

She subdued the urge to laugh out loud as he'd just compared himself to a dog's hindquarters. "You'll forgive me if I don't."

"Aye." Done with his inspection, he returned her hands to her lap. Unaccountably, she wished she *had* twisted her ankle. If the heat streaking up her arms was any indication, he'd have her legs warm for a month. "If it's guilt you seek to heap upon my head—"

"It isn't. I assure you. But you did ask..."

"So I did. Though it doesn't escape my notice that *asking* appears to yield results demanding does not, I vow I refuse to budge from your side until your lips share what you insist on keeping so closely guarded—that of how you came to be in such a predicament."

He termed her blindness a predicament? What an unusual word choice. She appreciated how very casual he was about it. "*I vow*," she gently mocked, "you're beginning to sound much like Harriet."

"Heaven forfend," he muttered darkly. "I'm more than double her age if I'm a day and certainly don't need to be sounding like a schoolroom chit, even one so entertaining. But come now. The others shall be returned by the evening meal and at this rate I'll count myself fortunate to have been granted the letters of your last name, much less a full explanation."

"I promise to convey those letters into your safekeeping before our host and hostess arrive and bombard you with more choice descriptors."

"Descriptors?"

"Ah...cork-brained simpleton being one of but a few."

"A reminder I could have gone all day without but I shall thank you for it nevertheless."

"Generous of you," she said, having more fun than she'd had during any conversation in recent memory.

"On the contrary, it is miserly you are, I'm beginning to see." He sighed as though sorely aggrieved. "'Tis this not the season of goodwill and charity? Can you not share some of your own without scoffing an idiotic imbecile? One who plays the court jester quite well without any help at all?"

"At least I have discovered one of your talents. Do you juggle too?"

"One of my talents? That of the fool, you mean?" He made a credible cannon-blast noise and jerked into her as if wounded. "Oh! A direct hit!"

Laughing as he plainly intended, Isabella considered how far she wanted to stretch her newfound bravado, having never had the occasion to flirt with a man before. And by now Isabella recognized full well what she was doing. Recognized it and was loving every second. Not for the first time since he'd joined her, she hoped the housekeeper was delayed in returning with the promised refreshments, having no wish to have their discourse interrupted. "Were I to answer your questions without quibble, do you then agree to answer mine?"

With an exaggerated, long-suffering air, he returned, "If I must, I must."

"You will tell me why you have such a reputation for..."

"Being unfeeling? Cold? Arrogant?"

"Though I'm tempted to let you go on for I find the enumeration of your faults quite illuminating, I was going to say *grumpy*."

He barked a laugh. "Then why didn't you?"

"I lacked the courage."

"One thing you do not lack, Miss Issybee— nay, I believe I prefer Issy*belle*—is courage.

Though the longer you keep me waiting, the more I begin to doubt that assessment."

It was exhilarating, bantering about with a lord—especially one so many found fearsome. Isabella only found him engaging. And appealing. And so many other things that if she let herself, she could easily forget what awaited her at the end of the holiday. Pushing away the unwelcome reminder, she said lightly, "So, you are in dire need of hearing how it happened?"

"Aye," he said dryly.

Some imp made her reply, "I couldn't keep up with your pace, my lord. My foot—"

"Not *that*, you vexing female, as you well know." His bluster only made her smile more. "Your sight. How did you lose it?"

"You know, I do believe you're the first person to ask it of me so directly. Most people either dance around the topic, as if my inability to see doesn't exist or they fall over themselves with so much solicitousness I'm smothered by it. But you..." She paused, unsure how to proceed.

How much did he want to know, truly?

How much did she want to share?

He retrieved her left arm and it was only

then that she became aware of how restless she'd grown, how her fingers had tangled in a loose strip of bandage she'd pulled free from the back of one hand. "Me?" he said. "I'm the nodcock who didn't even *notice* by damn—beg pardon."

He smoothed her palm and fingers over something solid and warm—his thigh? Her hand fluttered beneath his but Isabella made no move to retract it, consciously making an effort to relax her muscles against his hard flesh with every bit as much effort as she attempted to regulate her breathing.

"Pardon granted," she whispered. "Go on."

"I'm... I..." He shifted against her as though his limbs were all a rumpus. Much like her quivery midsection. "I'm— *Bloody hell.* I just noticed they seated you beneath...put us below..."

Eyes wide, she leaned toward him, seeking to understand. "What? The ceiling? Is something broken or not to your liking?" He growled and she gave a decisive nod as if everything were suddenly clear. "That's it...the hanging candelabra! I was placed beneath sputtering candles that have now burned out and earned your ire, but no... I don't smell any remnants of smoke. Do tell me, are we about to be set upon by a flock of rebellious wicks?"

"You think I'm so grumpy as to complain about a trifling chandelier?"

"Trifling? I daresay you would not call them so if the light they shed allowed you to see." Realizing what she'd said, she tacked on, "Which they do, if I'm not mistaken."

"You aren't," he groaned. "You have the right of it and I no doubt deserve to be bashed on the head with a heavy chandelier...only that is not what hangs above us."

"Then, pray, what is the source of your consternation? Did Mrs. Parksen guide me to a perilous location?"

"Perilous for my sanity," he muttered darkly. "We're sitting directly beneath a kissing bough."

"Noooo..." Oh, the possibilities that brought to mind...

"Yes. An emphatic *yes*."

Was he angry? She couldn't tell. "Yet had you not mentioned it, I would have remained oblivious."

"True."

Her lips tingled.

Her whole body burned.

A clock somewhere in the room ticked away the seconds.

Yet for Isabella, time stood still.

His touch along the back of her hand firmed. "I cannot help but notice you make no move to, ah...move."

Her breath whooshed out. "Nor do you."

Now what? Did he place his lips against her trembling own? Cup her cheek and smooth his thumb down her temple and get slapped for his efforts?

The innocent feel of her hand upon his thigh brought forth all manner of anything-but-innocent urges. Had since he'd secured it there.

By damn, if a slap was in the offing, he wanted to do significantly more than steal a simple kiss. "But I also want my bloody questions answered."

"Pardon?"

Reluctantly, Frost released her hand and stood. "Appears to me as though this particular kissing bough has been dedicated for our use, or at least that's what I'm deciding, given its propinquity and position."

He bit back a smile at her exclaimed, "Oh!",

hearing both disappointment—that he wasn't making use of it now, perhaps?—and anticipation—that he had definite plans to in the future—if he didn't miss his guess. Stretching, he freed the beribboned mistletoe. "I'll just pocket this beauty and we'll make use of it at a later date, shall we? Hmmm?"

Not that it would fit in his pocket, not without squashing it to a pulp, but she didn't need to know that. So he tossed it on the settee, out of her reach.

"But that's not how it works!"

Frost reseated himself, closer this time if that were possible. "I know full well how they work—"

"Of a certainty, a man like you would."

"What's that supposed to mean?" Exasperated with her now, he nudged her chin until she faced him fully, noting the flush on her cheeks and the impressive gash slicing through one eyebrow and up part of her forehead...last night's dangling curl had disguised the mark then this morning's bonnet had done the same. Noting too the spark glinting in her blinking eyes.

Stupidly, he sliced one hand in front of her. Nothing. Not a flinch nor a flicker. "Never mind that. How did you lose your sight?" He suspected the several-year-old scar told the story, but wanted to hear it from her. "I gather you haven't always been blind."

"Nooo," she sighed. "No. I..."

"I'm a brute for asking." Or demanding. But he didn't retract nor regret the need to know.

"No. Well, *yes*," she said amid a soft smile then ducked as if afraid he'd seen too much. "But that isn't why I hesitate."

Abruptly, she jerked her head up and stared straight at him. More precisely, within half an inch of straight at him. "Do you know, this is the first time I have been away from home since the accident, other than traveling to physicians and such?"

Frost shifted until his face was framed directly between those pale emerald peepers. "Why is that?"

Rather than respond, she shuttered her eyelids. Hiding from him?

"Isabella?"

"You asked how it happened," she said instead of answering his most recent question. "I was not yet Harriet's age..."

"A mere babe, then," he said, subduing the

gut-clenching sorrow he experienced at imagining this spirited woman suffering at any age. He manufactured a laugh for her benefit. "Ah yes, Harriet. I met the vivacious sprite soon after Ed became enamored of his lady wife. Harriet again entertained me at their wedding. Which you didn't attend. I would have remembered."

"That's...flattering of you to note. I think."

"It is," he confirmed then sought to soften it when he realized how pompous he sounded. "I mean, you may think it so."

"Glad am I to have your permission on the direction my thoughts take." Why was it her simple sentence only compounded his unintended pretentious air?

"I meant it as such. Flattering, I mean." How the deuce did she end up making *him* stumble around? "Are you always this evasive? You have yet to really tell me—"

"Wait." Her head snapped to the side, her entire body tensing. "Do you hear that?"

Only silence presented itself. "Hear what?"

"They're rehearsing!" She gripped the fabric of his jacket just beneath his shoulder, at once impassioned. "No one is returned yet, are they?"

Flummoxed at the wild change of topic, Frost's brows drew together as he puzzled her meaning...then finally...a distant howl resolved itself into the high-pitched screech of a horsehair bow scraping across catgut. "The musicians, you mean? And to answer your question, the rest of our party is still chasing after whatever items are on those blighted lists Lady Redford distributed." He patted his pocket and heard the crumple. "Appears I still have ours. Good tinder for the fire if you ask—"

"May we continue our discourse later, do you think? I'd like to...to...lie down and rest for a bit, I believe."

Lie down, his arse. She was lying right now, that much he knew, but to what end? "Certainly," he agreed with false equanimity, having no desire to relinquish her company. But he was good at reading the opposition and predicting their next move. The two of them might not be in a true battle but if it was a battle of wills—or wits—she wanted, he'd give it to her. "Let me escort you to your room."

"Oh, there's no need for that," she exclaimed with suspicious energy for one so suddenly exhausted, standing and smoothing her gown over her hips.

He'd wager his team of matched grays she had no inkling how very alluring the gesture, how very *lured* he was to ferret out her secrets. For some strange reason he wanted to be her confidant and much, much more.

Damn blasted Christmas spirit. It was blighting his soul with hope unlike any he'd known for years.

With a slight curtsy, she quit the room, leaving him slack-jawed at the poise and confidence with which she did so, gaining her bearings and stepping precisely from the settee. When her outstretched fingertips met the doorframe, she made a slight adjustment and sailed on through.

He was astonished. And impressed. "Deuced amazing."

Not only how well she got on but that he'd finally met a female he wanted to know more about, and for the second time in as many days, she'd abandoned him mid-conversation —and this one couldn't even *see* him frown.

Not that Frost felt as though he'd been frowning earlier. He was now, that was a certainty.

On silent feet, he followed, watching her trail one hand along the wall as she navigated the stairway and corridors of Redford Manor until coming upon the ballroom.

As graceful as an ethereal spirit, she slipped past the heavy double doors and disappeared inside without once making a sound —Frost knew because he was doing his damnedest to remain equally as quiet.

A second later he slipped inside after her.

With the drapes pulled shut and hanging candelabras and mounted wall sconces unlit, the cavernous room was dim. The only shaft of light came from the windows in the musicians' gallery overhead, the dedicated alcove concealed from direct view by a long curtain.

He waited by the door while his eyes adjusted. The moment they did, his heart caught. Frost knew he was being granted a vision few mortals ever had the fortune to behold—that of an angel in human form gliding across an empty floor...uninhibited, unencumbered by either her own—or society's—rigid standards.

Pure magic. Isabella's movements were pure magic. Keeping to the center of the room, which wasn't difficult given its enormous size, she swayed and stretched, skipped and soared, her body turning and twisting in ways he'd never dare conceive, much less imagine being a witness to, especially under what seemed clandestine circumstances.

He liked that, how watching her secret, sinuous dance, experiencing it with her—even without her knowledge—made it seem as if the two of them shared an illicit bond.

Though the more he observed, the more he realized she didn't so much dance as blend her body with the music. When one of the violinists botched a section and the entire quartet began the piece anew, she barely registered the interruption, her feet faltering but a moment before the sweeping, flowing motion of her limbs overtook her again.

Each time she spun near, he gazed upon the elation brimming from her face—the visage of pure, unadulterated joy, the exhilaration...the innocence. It pained him to watch.

Frost knew she counted herself alone, knew he violated her trust as much as he dishonored himself by remaining, but he could no more leave than sever his own tongue.

Her beauty, her grace...her spirit. They touched him as nothing had in almost twenty years. For some unaccountable reason, naught but the act of *watching* her joyous freedom expressed through uninhibited movement made him feel free, happy almost.

Nay, this wasn't mere happiness surging through his veins, exciting his heart and quickening his breath. Nothing so mediocre. This...*this* was the spirit of Christmas, somehow embodied in a sightless girl, that was causing him to see his own past—and future?—in ways he'd been blinded to previously.

His eyes stung from straining in the obscure light—any other reason was unfathomable. He closed them for a moment... imagining he was dancing with her, holding her; imagining she could *behold* him, unhindered by her lack of sight...

At the thought of embracing her again, his pulse leapt and his arms burned. Eyes blinked open...and still the vision that was Isabella continued to captivate.

Frost took a single step forward, intent on joining her.

But something made him hesitate and he stilled, reluctant to disrupt the scant minutes of liberty, to mar the freedom the music and private place afforded this unique woman, simply because of his selfishness to spend them with her.

He thought of her rebuff the prior night when he'd asked her to dance—demanded a dance, were he being honest. He thought of her unease after declining—and the look of longing he'd glimpsed on her features even as she pertly denied him.

He thought of their aborted conversation in the parlor, of how he still had no answers, and how she'd lied in order to claim this time for herself. To be alone. To be free.

But most of all, he thought of the countless berries on that kissing bough still sitting on the settee.

He thought of her mouth and how she'd blushed.

He thought of the ten days of Christmas still to come—the eleven nights including this one—and how for the first time since Althea died he wasn't dreading tomorrow. Was, in fact, anticipating it with all the undue enthusiasm of an untried buck.

As silently as he'd entered, Frost exited the ballroom with but one destination in mind.

The settee in the parlor.

5

A FESTIVE BERRY CHANGES HAND

"WOULD you be gracious enough to explain how I was to 'fully participate' in a searching game?" Isabella asked Anne from her reclined position—foot propped on two pillows—in the corner of the formal drawing room where she'd been carried after partaking a simple repast in her bedchamber.

Isabella felt a complete charlatan but couldn't bring herself to put lie to Lord Frost-wood's claim that she'd injured her ankle. Neither was she accustomed to such subterfuge. Feigning an injury niggled her conscience—but not enough to confess all.

"You conversed with Frost, did you not?"

"Yessss…" Isabella trailed off, uncomprehending how speaking with the engaging gentleman had anything to do with participating in Anne's holiday fun. She heard the trod of feet and the low rumble of approaching conversation and realized other guests were joining them, dinner officially over.

"Well, dearest, that was *exactly* what I had planned for you. Though the fall was completely *unplanned*, I assure you."

Isabella lowered her voice, thankful no one had yet made their way to her corner. "You contrived all of this to what end? What can you expect by pairing me with—"

"*Expect*ations, my dear. You have the right of it—expectations."

"You think to gain a marriage proposal from your machinations?" Her stomach slid to her feet—actually, beneath her posterior, seated as she was—at the fanciful notion. "I fear you are destined for disappointment, then." So was Isabella, but her friend need not know that. "You're aware of what Father intends for me come February—"

"Pshaw! He's a looby if he thinks we're going graciously along with those plans."

Isabella pleaded, "Stop, please. You are married now—" She placed a hand in the vicinity of her friend's belly and felt the gently rounded expansion. "With a family of your own to contend with. Spinning castles for your girlhood friend—"

"Is exactly what I will do," Anne concluded with temerity, "and they *aren't* fairy castles, dearest. You haven't seen how he looks at you. I have."

Though she feared her sudden smile might give away her reluctant longing, Isabella refused to comment, firming her lips into a straight line the moment she noticed their upward tilt.

"You shall have to trust me," Anne added. "Newly married I may be, but there are some things a woman just knows. And I daresay, if we can keep him from haring off before Epiphany, you'll have Frost so charmed he won't want to leave your presence. Ever."

———— ◦◦ ————

THAT NIGHT, damn and blast, instead of another course of dancing as he'd anticipated, everyone made a great show of being judged on how well they'd gathered the items on their list. Damn and blast because he'd intended to *ask* Isabella to accompany him onto the floor, double damn and blast once he realized she wouldn't be able to join him, not without keeping up appearances, thanks to his inept handling of this morning's debacle.

After excessive jollity and wassail drinking —he'd still yet to take a sip—Harriet and her partner, one of the stuffy-nosed Fairfax chits, were deemed the winners and rather than outwardly deride every ridiculous reminder of the season as he'd always done in the past, and fully meant to do today, Frost found himself grinning along with the winning team as they made a great show of displaying their bounty, which ranged the gamut from a squawking Christmas goose—neck intact and covered with an elaborately tied yet trailing red ribbon—to a hand-fashioned manger scene complete with hay and a carved baby Jesus.

Frost's mystifying contentment only increased when he observed the reverence with which Isabella inspected the Nativity, her still-bandaged hands moving with care as she brushed her fingertips over the pieces—after the loudly honking goose made its displeasure at being petted quite clear.

The festive atmosphere was downright infectious, and Frost was stunned to realize he was in what could be termed nothing but high spirits, especially when he directed Ed's attention to the little morsels the goose had deposited on the rug.

High spirits indeed, until he noticed that Isabella's mishap was being laid firmly at his doorstep—where it rightfully belonged, but still!—judging by the hostile looks aimed his way and how she was fussed and hovered over, making it nigh impossible to reach her side, much less exchange one of the berries weighing heavily in his pocket. For her kiss.

Ah well. Ten more nights, he had, to further his cause. Exactly what that was, he'd yet to admit to himself.

Perhaps more importantly than the number of nights—especially considering he hadn't decided how long to stay—was determining how soon an evening of dancing would once again grace the schedule and how soon Isabella's phantom sprain might heal.

Damn and blast again. At being told to herd the damn blasting goose straight to the kitchens, the usually laughing Harriet sprite looked as though she'd come down with the mulligrubs.

———————— ◦◦◦ ————————

"THANK YOU, sir, for your exceptional escort," Isabella told Mr. Gregory when he informed her they'd reached her bed-chamber door. She'd pleaded fatigue after such an eventful day though in truth she was simply desirous of some time alone. "It is most gallant of you to leave your card game for the chore."

In actuality, he'd tripped over himself—and the squawking goose Harriet refused to relinquish to a servant—in his effort to be the one to carry Isabella to the guest wing. She felt a total fraud. But more than that, a *disappointed* total fraud, for Mr. Gregory was certainly not the man she'd hoped would volunteer for the task.

"Think nothing of it. I have had you in my arms through a good many twists and turns of Redford's monstrous abode, the least you can do is call me Simon." And if he knew what monstrous dowry she *didn't* have, Isabella was certain he wouldn't be so eager to pursue such familiarity.

After settling her slowly upon her feet and ensuring she could make it the rest of the way on her own—Isabella insisted she could—he lifted her hand and pressed it against his chest.

"Good night, lovely Lady Isabella."

Though flattered by his focused attention, she squirmed inside at the unwanted blandishment. Any other time, she was certain she would have delighted in his company, for he had some of the most unusual interests and could entertain with any number of tales. How many other people of her acquaintance—not that she had many to number, not until *this* Christmas—had a propensity to work in a laboratory, making things explode?

It wasn't his fault he wasn't *the* person she wanted to be with. And for all of that, his attention wasn't as welcome as it otherwise would have been.

Isabella breathed easier when he gave her fingers a light clasp and moved to relinquish her hand. But rather than place it upon the doorknob, he brought it to his lips and blew a kiss over her bare fingertips. "Unless the term *good night* is precipitous? Would you care to extend the evening with additional conversation? I could ring for a maid to act as chaperone or carry you back to—"

"Ah, Isabella, the very person I was looking for," another voice called down the hallway, causing both relief at the welcome interruption and rapid respiration over who it was. Better still, the smooth voice prompted her erstwhile suitor to release her hand. "Lady Redford bid me to consult with you on a matter of great import, if I may," Lord Frostwood finished just as he reached her side. "Gregory."

"Frost," Mr. Gregory returned in a chilly tone she couldn't help but notice. Upset at having his overture thwarted? Or simply not fond of the other man?

Regardless of his feelings on the matter, *she* was delighted. Though the tension thickened once the three of them stood there.

"Certainly, my lord," she said as though engaging two men in the hallway outside her bedchamber was a frequent occurrence. She then nodded in the direction she sensed Mr. Gregory remained, whether reluctant to leave her in Lord Frostwood's safekeeping or simply reluctant to *leave* she knew not which and didn't care. *Be gone with you and quickly*, she urged in her mind while saying aloud with what she hoped was proper reserve, "Thank you again for your kindness this evening."

"Yes, well, *ahem*," Mr. Gregory stammered a moment. "Good night then."

Spaced footfalls told of his hesitant retreat. When the sound disappeared altogether, Lord Frostwood blew out a loud breath. "Was beginning to think the bounder would never find the end of the hallway."

She bit her lip to subdue the smile that threatened. "For shame. He was being all that was gentlemanly, I assure you."

"What's shameful is watching the jolterhead's lame attempts at pawing over your injuries. How goes the last one, Issybelle?"

As he accompanied this perplexing question with a light caress across several fingers on her right hand, all coherent thoughts flew from her mind. "Last one? Attempts?"

"Last injury. I saw Harriet's ghastly behaving goose peck at your fingers."

He'd been close enough to see that? And he'd taken to calling her Issybelle? Heat blossomed through her; only her dear mama had ever called her that. "I find it interesting that you would inquire about that *now* yet show no interest when the goose decided my fingertips were for nibbling."

"Mayhap not all interest can be shown."

What was that supposed to mean? "Well then, I thank you for your query and am pleased to impart that I suffer no ill effects from attempting to befriend a misbehaving goose. Although how a newly leashed goose put upon display in a boisterous drawing room is *supposed* to behave if not ghastly, I haven't an inkling."

"And your interest in Gregory? Have you an inkling as to that?" Lord Frostwood fired the words at her. "He was showing his in you plainly enough all evening. What is yours for him?"

"Simon? I only just met him."

"You only just met me."

"Then should you not be inquiring about my interest in you?"

"Undeniably I should, but that would require a measure of bravery I do not yet possess." He stroked a finger across the back of her hand again. "Especially after such an imperfect beginning. Shall I tell you instead of my interest in you?"

She pressed her lips together to keep from shouting, *But of course I am curious about your interest in me, you clunch! Think you I do not notice and am not baffled by it?* Showing such exuberance wouldn't do. Not at all.

"I see the words you refuse to loose flitting across your face. I shall assume your silence equates to curiosity then, hmm?" He took a firmer hold of the pecked-upon fingers and brought her arm up between them, caressing his thumb lightly over her skin.

Her hand trembled within his. "Please do."

Yet before he did, he released her. Dratted gnats. "Ah, but how can one answer aloud that which one has yet to admit to themselves?"

The breath she hadn't realized she held whooshed out on a groan. "You are the most perplexing fellow."

"Perplexing in an intriguing way, might I hope? Or perplexing in an annoying way? I would hate to find I cause you any manner of annoyance especially since I seem to find myself in remarkably high spirits any time you're near."

"An intriguing way, you scoundrel, for forcing such a confession from me." *For re-*

leasing my hand when I'd just come to long for more.

"Scoundrel? You wound me mightily."

"Yes, *scoundrel*, and I daresay one with such experience could not be wounded by anything I might utter."

"Then perchance you overestimate my experience or do not honor your own opinion sufficiently."

Had she possibly distressed him? She laughed at the absurdity of such a thought. "Nay. One as strong and sure as you is not to be affected by anything I might say."

"Hmm. Strong?" He sounded pleased.

"So you'll take that over scoundrel? Of course *strong*. You did carry me across a significant portion of the outer estate today and up a number of stairs without once showing any manner of undue exertion, did you not?"

"Aye, and Gregory carried you to your door." The last was growled.

Could that be jealousy she heard? What a wondrous thought—however implausible. Not jealousy, surely. More in line with rakish bravado. "Then mayhap you should have been closer when I expressed the desire to retire."

He leaned in. She knew because the heady

scent of sandalwood and man suddenly surrounded her more intently than before. "Much as I am now?"

It was hard to breathe when one feared the act would bring their bosom into direct contact with another's chest. Especially a male chest. Especially *this* particular male chest. Be that as it may, Isabella couldn't stop inhaling him, taking him in down to her toes and learning his scent...memorizing everything about this wickedly wonderful encounter.

Wicked? Should she be thinking such a thing?

How could she think anything else when it was all that swirled within her—wicked, wanton thoughts no maiden should ever entertain, but entertain them she did, which prompted her to ask, "Um...what if someone comes along and sees me *standing* here with you?" *Sees you standing so close we're practically sharing my slippers?* "Would that not put lie to our injured-ankle claim?"

"They will not." His words contained every bit the caress his fingers delivered upon her cheek. "I took it upon myself to induce Harriet to stand sentry at the entrance to the guest wing."

A picture of Harriet and her beribboned goose guarding the way flashed in Isabella's mind...honking and flapping wings and pecking at potential intruders—only with Harriet flapping arms in lieu of wings and abstaining from any pecking. The fanciful image didn't lessen the sensations streaking across her cheek one iota. "But her goose?"

"That's where I was earlier. Outside with Harriet, finding a secure spot for her new pet to bed down in a corner of the stables. Ed refused, saying the only place that goose was going was down his gullet, and I couldn't stand by and suffer the look of woe on her face when she realized her friend was truly meant for the dinner table. I gather Ed indulged her whims last year and abstained from Christmas goose; thought she'd mature beyond her fowl fascination by now." He left off stroking her cheek and settled one broad, heavy hand upon her shoulder. "Promised her I'd find a home for the wretched thing tomorrow—that was the inducement—if she helped ensure an empty hallway and moment of privacy once we returned and found you gone."

"It's been vastly longer than a moment, my lord."

"And you weren't the only one nipped by that dam— Ah, pardon me, that *deuced* goose."

"Deuced goose," she managed with a smile, in spite of the thrilling warmth his hand caused to trickle through her body. "I may need to add that one to my repertory."

"You refer to your earlier exclamation of 'dratted gnats'?"

"Heard that, did you?"

"I did indeed. Care to share what others you have coined for your own?"

"No I do not, for they aren't suited for genteel conversation." What would he think of her should he overhear *damned lamb* or *poxed fox*? Not that she ever said them out loud, not ordinarily. "But there is something I would appreciate should you share it with me."

"You have but to name it."

"Can you..." His scrutiny warmed her face and she looked off toward the Harriet-ensured empty hallway. Oh, would that she could see him too!

"Can I what?" His husky tones made her vibrate inside.

"Can you explain why you would choose to sequester yourself entertaining me when such a vast array of amusements proceed elsewhere? Do you not long to be with your friends?"

"Sooo..." Easily could she hear the smile in his voice. One finger edged beneath her chin and directed her face back toward his. "You find me entertaining, do you?"

"Lord Frostwood!" She'd never been a sauce box before, couldn't believe she was being so bold now. Isabella knew their enthralling association would go nowhere once Twelfth Night signaled the end to this wondrous, magical holiday. And while part of her was loath to surrender even a second of his company, the more sedate, demure part—the stifled self she portrayed at home—thought it best to shoo him away before she became any more enchanted. "I am used to solitude, I assure you, my lord. You need not sacrifice your holiday attempting to engage and amuse the quiet wallflower in the corner."

"How can you describe yourself thusly?"

"I only give voice to the facts." A new thought occurred, one that threatened to put a pall over their entire exchange. "Did Lord Redford persuade you to—"

"Nay, he did not!" Frost said with such vehemence she could do naught but believe. "I spend time at your side because I choose to. It is not some dull swift's errand I'm on. You are a most confounding wench to broach such a dismal topic, particularly when I had different things in mind."

"Oh. That's right. You searched me out at Anne's behest. Pray, what is her message?" Though it didn't matter. Truly, she suspected nothing could elevate her mood any more than it was now. He *liked* spending time with her.

"Eh?"

Even his grunts sounded smooth and inviting, any noise he made or tone he chose to employ swirling into her ears, sliding down her spine and causing her toes to fair dance in her slippers. Pished fish, but he made her equilibrium go all higgledy piggledy. Isabella scooted one foot backward until her heel touched the door. Feeling more secure, she prompted, "Matter of great importance, my lord? I believe that's what you claimed."

"I lied," he said promptly. "Rotten thing to do, but there you have it. Dare I hope you have no great aversion to liars?"

How did one answer a question like that? Of course she had an aversion to liars. Didn't everyone? "Mmm...I'm certain liars, much like sinners, deserve our charity and forgiveness especially at this time of year."

She thought she heard a snort of laughter. "Well said. Did you enjoy your trip to Nod?"

"My trip to Nod?" She breathed deeply, inhaling him again.

"Your nap. This afternoon, remember? You needed to rest, if I recall correctly. Directly amidst our conversation."

Where were you seated earlier? she wanted to ask, having wondered all through the merriment after dinner. It was peculiar in the extreme, thinking she felt his gaze upon her person but being in no position to ask anyone for confirmation. Nor was she in a position to ask now. She blushed, recalling how intently she'd listened for *his* voice among all the others, blushed more fiercely, realizing he'd sought out this private moment with her. And admitted it, along with his interest in her—at least she thought he had—which only made her burn hotter.

He stepped closer. She heard the rustle of his clothing, sensed him along every inch of her being.

Instinctively, she retreated. Her back bumped into the door.

"Your face reddens, dear Isabella. Does your conscience perhaps trouble you?"

Her conscience? Nay, but his nearness...

"Ah well, mayhap now isn't the time for confessions, eh?"

"That's an odd thing to say."

"At least it's not a command," he quipped then, before she could respond, he ordered, "Close your eyes."

"What?" Why were they whispering?

"Close your eyes."

She did, just as he placed something against her bandaged palm, curled her fingers around it and brought her hand to his chest. "Push me away if I be too bold."

What? she thought again then could think no more for his lips were on hers, warm and solid and rubbing back and forth. Slowly, enticingly...causing her to murmur in her throat, to purse her lips in response. To rise up on her toes and press more firmly against the hard length of his body.

"Ah yes," he rasped against her mouth. Then the teasing exploration changed tenor as he leaned into her and took her lips more fully.

The back of her head thumped against the

door when his tongue licked its way across the seam of her lips.

She gasped and just as quickly he was gone —his body at least, for she could still hear his breathing. It was every bit as harsh as her own.

"Dream on me, Issybelle."

"*On* you?"

"All night long..." And he placed one last, lingering kiss to her forehead.

Then he was gone. For real this time.

Leaving her standing in the hallway, her heart threatening to take flight, her lips throbbing as if they'd never calm, her forehead practically glowing.

And her fingers clutched around a single mistletoe berry.

6

A DREARY MORNING MADE FESTIVE

Wings fluttered and she thought, Let it snow...

———◦∞◦———

AT THE UNGODLY hour of a quarter before dawn, Frost came across a maid in the candlelit breakfast room. "What are you doing, pray?"

He'd always been one to rise with the sun but hadn't expected to chance upon a young servant moving things about that didn't need moving. A chair previously aligned was now intentionally skewed, and eating utensils that belonged in a tray were instead clutched in her hand.

At his query, she startled and every piece of flatware clanged to the floor.

He waited for the clatter to die down then asked dryly, "You're not helping yourself to Redford's silver, now are you?"

"Never, milord! Lady Redford tasked me with rightin' things for Lady Isabella." As the girl spoke, she put the fallen utensils in the wash bin and retrieved three new pieces. With hands that shook, he noticed. The girl cast him a quick look then babbled on. "She tends to break her fast 'fore anyone else thinks to stir, she does. I make it so things are always in the same place for her. 'Tis all I'm doin' now, I promise, milord."

"You're telling me she serves herself?" he asked suspiciously, seeing the row of warming trays on the adjacent wall, surprised they'd be filled this early. "Does she not simply request what she wants and have it brought from the kitchens?"

"Oh no. Lady Isabella never asks for anything partic'lar, says how she enjoys sampling whatever Cook fixes, but she does like holdin' her own plate as I tell her about each dish. Says she can tell by how heavy it gets whether I went and made her portions too big. She doesn't want the extra goin' to waste, you see."

He was beginning to. Beginning to realize the female his body and mind were equally attracted to had hidden depths that he very much wanted to plumb. Not wanting to be wasteful? That sounded much like the independent young woman he'd enjoyed conversing with—and kissing—the day before.

Frost forced his posture to relax for the explanation was a plausible one and he wanted to put the anxious maid at ease. Nor was he above questioning this forthcoming servant about his new enchantment. "Lady Redford charged you? Did the Lady Isabella not bring servants or a maid of her own to see to her care? A chaperone?"

"Nay, milord. Arrived alone, she did."

Alone? How unusual. "How long ago was that?"

"Nigh on three weeks or thereabouts."

Remarkable, that she'd gained such familiarity about the place in so little time.

The girl slid her eyes toward the door. Ready to escape his clutches no doubt.

"Two more things if you will..."

"Milord?"

"Is anyone else assigned to assist Isabella?" And if he shouldn't be referring to her with such informality, then what of it? How could one feel *formal* toward the most compelling lass they had ever chanced across?

"Just Sally, as a lady's maid, fixin' her gowns and hair and such."

"And you? What other duties have you been given on her behalf?"

"I keep all the furniture just so an' clear the hallways thrice daily, makin' sure no one's left anything on the floors or blockin' her footpaths."

"She moves about much, does she?"

"Yes, milord."

He took pity on the young girl and smiled with as much charm as he could manage, eyebrows flat, dimples engaged. "Thank you... your name?"

"Lizzie, milord." She bobbed a curtsy.

"Well, Lizzie, I appreciate all that you're doing for Isabella. Carry on."

She flashed him a bright grin now that the inquisition was over and he wasn't marching her off to Newgate for stealing. "She's lovely, milord, Lady Isabella is. Everyone below stairs says so. In form and fact. 'Tis been a real treat, it has, helpin' her an' such."

And it would be a *real treat* to share the falling snowflakes with her, Frost decided after a glance out the window brought the idea to mind, the sun's hidden rays stretching sufficiently for him to make out the swirling flakes.

Taking the stairs two at a time back the way he'd just come, Frost raced toward the guest wing where everyone else had been abed, for he now had reason to believe one miss Lady Isabella would no longer be occupying hers.

Seconds later, subduing his eagerness and his voice, he rapped his knuckles against her door twice. "It's Frost."

After a moment the door opened a crack, just enough to reveal a sliver of porcelain cheek and ear. Her hair was draped over her shoulder, he saw with a tightening in his gut, not yet arranged for the day. A pink dressing gown covered said shoulder, and just as he was pondering what else—if anything—might lie beneath, she queried, "Lord Frostwood? Are you there?"

"Aye," he answered as quietly as she had but with more urgency, unwilling to rouse any nearby guests yet not wanting to dally lest the snowfall come to an end. "Get dressed and bundle up. There's something I would show you out—"

"*Show* me?" He saw the curve of her inviting mouth when she turned to speak through the crack.

He laughed softly. "My apologies, but what can one expect from a cork-brained simpleton? *Experience* with me, then. Please?"

"A 'please' from the man who issues the order to bundle up? This must be serious indeed."

He growled. "Serious punishment if you do not comply, woman. Now attire yourself properly and let's be off." She opened the door a fraction more and he realized what he'd thought a dressing gown was in truth day dress. One sans chemisette, he was pleased to note, giving him an enjoyable view of the top of her bosom. "Good. Very good. Now—"

"What manner of punishment, my lord?" The odd inflection in her voice drew his gaze upward to find her evaluating him, her glinting eyes banked for once. There was no possibility she knew where *his* had settled, was there? "I'm most curious," she continued, and her tone conveyed her seriousness, "would you banish me from your presence? Exile me to a convent, an institution? Or merely lock me in my room with neither food nor water?"

"Only if I locked myself in there with you."

Her cheeks flamed. "For shame."

He stood there, taking in her blushing response to his pert reply. Appreciating her pert nose and farther down, her pert br— "Ahem. Yes...well, that's me. A shameless, experienced rake. Or so you have indicated a time or two—which is not entirely accurate, by the way. But if you insist on debating word choices and decline to accept my invitation—for that's what it is, you know—alas, I shall be forced to enjoy the dancing snowflakes alone. What a pity, do you not—"

"Snowflakes?" Her eyes once again sparkled like rain-drenched holly.

"Mind you, they weren't respectably large nor plentiful when I saw them just now so I cannot guarantee how long they'll last, but yes, *snowflakes*. Meandering down from yon clouded sky this very moment."

As if that knowledge lent steel to her spine, she came to attention. "Wonderful! You *wonderful* man!" Her smile made him feel ten feet tall. "I'll be but a trice!" And she snapped the door shut against his nose.

Ow!

Damn. He'd have a bruised conk by nuncheon.

It was no more than he deserved, though, given how he'd peered over her head and into her room, seeking more information about the intriguing, interesting, exceptionally enchanting miss Isabella.

———— ∘◦∘ ————

"WHAT A GLORIOUS BEGINNING TO A NEW DAY!" Isabella didn't care that her hair was stuffed haphazardly into the nearest bonnet at hand and her ears were close to freezing, didn't care that she'd exhibited no decorum whatsoever when Lord Frostwood came knocking upon her door—now *that* had truly been a glorious beginning—didn't care that she'd made no effort to disguise her excitement in the unexpected outdoor excursion...

Didn't care that she was falling for—had already fallen, if one took into account her meeting with the ground yesterday—a completely inappropriate man. Inappropriate not because of who he was, but because of who *she* was. Inappropriate because of where her future lay. But for once she didn't give a fig for that either—not now. All she cared about at the moment was the powerful man at her side with his strong arm about her back, guiding her over the manicured lawn, "Crisp and brown, complements of Old Man Winter," he'd just told her.

"I don't care if we trod within a muddy ditch," she said truthfully, feeling the thin layer of moisture seep inside her slippers with every crunching step. "Don't believe I'd care if my feet turn to blocks of ice—this is worth it a thousand times over."

"I promise to whisk you inside ere your feet freeze in truth. I don't need another mishap of yours laid at my doorstep. The ones I was responsible for yesterday are quite enough, I assure you."

"How you go on, Lord Frostwood. No one blames you for my clumsiness." While she spoke, a flurry of wind blew a flake or two past her lips and into her mouth. Isabella was instantly reminded of the sensation of his tongue gliding toward that same destination

the night before. She ducked to hide her increased awareness of him.

"Yes of course, because everyone can easily
see what a gummy gollumpus you are," he
chided with no little irony, leading them in another direction. "Isabella, clumsy you most
certainly are not."

"You say that with such certainty given how
short our acquaintance. I cannot help but
think you champion me simply because you
think it's required as a gentleman."

He coughed softly. "Yes, well...ahem. I will
grant my surety of your gracefulness comes
not from a wish to curry favor, nor do I choose
to continue defending myself against your un-
founded accusation and attempt to convince
you of the truth of my observation, for indeed I
have something of greater interest to share
with you."

"I am upon thorns and needles awaiting
whatever it might be."

"Woman, you mock me thoroughly." He
sounded so aggrieved she could do naught but
unsuccessfully muffle a laugh. "You'll be happy
to note the flakes are growing larger and what's
more, they aren't that beautiful color of soot
one tends to find in London."

"So...big white fluffy ones are coming down now?"

"Aye, I ordered them to. How else could I shield our excursion from any curious onlookers? You must agree, traipsing the grounds isn't recommended for one with so egregiously a wounded ankle."

"Even the heavens obey your orders? Then they are much better behaved than I." She curved her elbow around his forearm so she could tug the glove free from her opposite hand. The gloves had been on her nightstand when she retired last evening though Isabella was certain she'd searched there initially. Discounting the perplexing mystery, she held up a bare palm, having removed the bandages that morning, and laughed when the cold chill met her flesh. "Guide me, oh He Who Rules the Weather," she intoned. "I'll catch some of these prodigious flakes you commanded into existence."

She expected him to direct her with words. Instead, he cupped his large hand beneath hers and tilted and swayed her arm—and their aligned bodies—bringing her flesh into contact with wispy bits of icy nothing. Again and again.

Isabella laughed when several delicate flakes hit her palm, eager to savor each moment of this spectacular morning. The flakes soon melted into a freezing drop that slid toward her wrist. Her entire arm came alive as never before—or perhaps that was his nearness, enlivening her very existence. "This is lovely. I haven't been outside in years."

"Not outside?" He sounded astonished.

"Not like this." She relinquished her hold on his forearm and spun in a slow circle, confident he wouldn't have allowed the move had the way not been clear. "Glorious! Glorious!"

Isabella raised her face to the sky, squinted then blinked when gossamer shards of ice hit her eyes, and laughed some more. *Free*, she realized. She hadn't felt this free since The Accident and resulting...imprisonment imposed by her father.

But *this*? Racing outside to enjoy an early morning snowfall with Lord Frostwood? Pure Christmas magic with a magical lord, one she'd give anything to see...

Blinking incipient tears now as well as snow, she drew the bracing air into her lungs and spun faster, allowing her feet to cross in front of each other, whipping her body round and round. It was the closest she could come to running full-out. Her chest strained with the effort, her head reeled from the motion.

One foot slid on the icy ground.

But Frost was there in an instant, sweeping her against his chest and brandishing his lips across hers.

Mouths pressed intimately together, her feet dangling in the air, his arms secure about her waist and hers wound over his shoulders, Isabella surrendered to the man before her, gave everything she had to matching his kiss, unwilling to think of all the reasons why she shouldn't.

HER LIPS TASTED of a fresh spring morning. Of new life and pure innocence. And that's what stopped him—the innocence.

She hadn't a clue how much deeper he wanted to take their kiss, how he'd envisioned taking her to bed with him last night, baring her body before his hungry gaze and showing her all the passion he'd kept locked inside until chancing across an unassuming, utterly beguiling miss...

Passion that now threatened to rise to the

surface, heating him to boiling on a cold winter's day with nothing more than the taste of innocent frosty lips beneath his own.

With a groan, he tore his mouth from hers and lowered her feet to the ground. Breathing hard and attempting to mask it, Frost said lightly, "There now, we can't go ruining the perfect morning by having you take a tumble."

"A *tumble*, my lord?" She licked her lips, tasting him one last time if he wasn't mistaken. It was while watching those glistening, now-swollen lips, while watching snowflakes land upon them and leaning in to kiss her again—his conscience be damned—that her words registered, as did his own.

"Blast and da— Dratted gnats! Take a tumble, as in fall, not tumble as in...the other. Blast!"

Flushed pink but with a saucy smile and her arms still about his neck, she rocked backward on one leg then came forward again until their chests almost touched. "Gratified am I, you made that clear."

Though it seemed reluctant to him, she took her arms down and stepped away. "Although...should I behave as I ought, I would now be taking to the snow in a swoon and crying, 'Lord Frostwood, you dastard! What if someone chances by?'"

He fought the urge to take her into his arms again. "Then I would behave as I ought *not* and assure you, 'There's no one around, my dear. And if there were, I wouldn't care.'"

As if embracing the role, she magnified her pseudo-protest, pressing both hands to her throat and exclaiming, "But... We can't! We shouldn't!"

Convincing himself as well as her, Frost stood his ground in the increasing snowfall and demanded in a mock-gruff voice, "Whyever not? There's a spray of mistletoe overhead, I'll have you know."

"There is?" she asked in her regular tone, lowering her arms. "Oh. I didn't realize we were under a tree."

They weren't.

"Of course there is," he lied without qualm. What was it about her that drove him to do so? He'd never been one to spout clankers before —not since embellishing nonexistent holidays at school.

Frost quickly fished a berry from his pocket—he'd had the forethought to stash several there earlier—and made a great show of stretching toward the cloud-studded sky, which was all that hung over them at present. "Here—don't bite down now."

He placed the white berry between her lips then covered them with his own lest she swallow the damn thing. The only thing he wanted in her mouth that didn't belong there was his tongue.

What was he thinking? His tongue *did* belong there!

Sucking the berry into his mouth and tucking it alongside his cheek and out of the way, he applied himself to convincing her of the truth of that thought—how very much his tongue *belonged* upon her person. Inside her person.

How very much he was beginning to believe he belonged inside her heart. As she was swiftly melting his.

7

A SLEW OF FESTIVE
BERRIES

———◆◆◆———

"YOU ARE RETURNED from delivering your new feathered friend?" Ed had the audacity to inquire when Frost marched up the drive after his errand later the same day.

The wet clouds had departed and the sun now sparked off the three inches of snow that blanketed the ground from that morning, very few footprints—save his own and a webbed pair alongside—marring its pristine condition.

"Stuff it," he said. "Have you any idea the look a farmer bestows upon a man who pays him *not* to butcher prime livestock? 'Queer titled pudding-head', I think I heard him mutter."

Ed laughed then nodded toward the boisterous gathering spilling out of the house, Harriet in the lead. "She hasn't stopped singing your praises since last night. You spoil her and she'll think all men are so kind."

"Kind, eh?" Frost wasn't used to hearing himself described as such. "Girls are meant to be spoiled."

"And women? What say you there?" Ed asked with a quizzical expression.

"Depends upon the woman. Any particular one you're inquiring about?"

"What happened to your nose? It looks larger than usual...and it's turning purple if I'm not mistaken."

It *felt* larger than usual, thanks to its ill-timed collision with a certain female's bedchamber door. Felt as if he wore a damn elephant on his face. "I'd rather talk about women."

"Who wouldn't, old chap?"

"Frost!" Bundled to the gills, Anne rushed over, looking much like her guests if more solemn of countenance. "I owe you my humblest apologies, my lord, for my outburst yesterday."

"Nay, you do not. Particular bits of information would have stood me in good stead, I cannot help but think, but all is well."

"But I called you an imbecile. A...simpleton."

"I'm quite clear on that, my lady, for your colorful expressions still resound in my ears —'cork-brained simpleton' I believe it was." She paled but held his gaze. "Think no more of it. Nor shall I. Where is Lady Isabella?" he asked with as much indifference as he could manage, noticing she'd yet to join the others now rolling snowballs and tromping through unblemished clouds of white.

"Upstairs resting."

He knew what that meant. "Dancing again this evening?"

"Thought you didn't favor doing the pretty," Ed put in.

Frost arched one eyebrow but didn't respond. Didn't need to when Lady Redford smiled brightly. "Why, yes. We told the musicians to play a waltz or two so it should be grand fun."

"Yes...grand." He turned to go inside.

"You're not joining us?" she called after him. "Don't you want to lead one side against Ed's team?"

"I'll join you tonight, but for now I believe I shall go in and rest myself. One can only endure so much honking and snow-bright revelry before they must retreat." He touched the brim of his hat and continued on.

"Ah...Nick, my boy?"

At the first step, he paused and looked over his shoulder at Ed.

"There's a feather or two affixed to your...posterior."

Lovely. Blasted lovely.

Heading up the stairs, he brushed a hand over his arse and flicked off the offending feathers, all the while wondering why the action only made him smile.

⬥

"Do my eyes deceive me or is that a Christmas angel dancing her way by?"

"Lord Frostwood?" Isabella yelped, and skidded to a halt.

"In the flesh."

"You gave me a fright."

Frost didn't doubt it, given how he'd not only found her flying through a back corridor on two healthy feet, but more importantly, given where he suspected she was heading. "Didn't hear me, hmm? Should I oblige by stringing a jangling harness round my neck?"

"'Tis not necessary, my lord." And just when he thought she was turning up stiff and reluctant to banter further, given how their most recent encounter culminated in the exchange of cold berries and heated kisses, she surprised him by adding, "I believe a few jingling bells tied at the end of your neckcloth shall suffice."

He laughed. "Wench."

"Scoundrel." she returned just as quickly then her brow furrowed. "You sound a trifle odd. You haven't picked up Miss Fairfax's snuffles, have you?"

"Nay." He wasn't about to tell her he'd been snooping over her shoulder. "Mayhap 'tis simply a reaction to goose feathers. Now where are you bound so swiftly? I shall offer my arms as escort." Without giving her time to refuse, he scooped her into his embrace and hefted her close. "Your ankle, you know."

"Oh do I. It appears I have much to thank it

for. But are you not expected elsewhere? I'm told the battlements are choosing sides for a massive snow strike before dinner."

He fancied he felt the rapid flutter of her heart thumping in time with his. "Nay. I told our zealous hosts I needed to rest after my goose-housing mission."

"And do you?"

"Need to rest? Only my back against this wall." He suited action to words, for he had no wish to release her or travel from the secluded hallway.

Isabella knew she should insist he put her down. Their interactions to date were wholly improper. To the devil with proprieties, she thought, choosing instead to curve her arm across the wide expanse of his shoulders and take him to task for another matter entirely. "Do you always brush aside the truth with such cavalier disregard?"

"Do you?" he surprisingly retorted.

"Certainly not! But we aren't talking about me."

"Oh no? I thought we were discussing you —your ears, my neck...your ankles, my arms..."

"Obtaining a forthright response from you is more difficult than me sighting in and downing a buck in one shot."

"Another accurate volley. My dear lady, with or without working top lights, you see more clearly than the rest of us, I vow. So you'd like to know whether I'm in the habit of disregarding the truth?"

She swung one foot while her fingertips brushed across the fine texture of his tailcoat. The fit was superb; the quality unmistakable. Her fascination with the muscles cording his shoulder most inappropriate! "I most assuredly would. As it seems a disturbingly frequent habit."

He took a moment's forethought before replying, she was pleased to note. "I am generally the most forthright of fellows. Appears 'tis something about being desirous of your company that causes imperfections in my character to come to the fore."

"Imperfections, Lord Frostwood?" she asked nonchalantly, hoping to disguise how very much the continued references bothered her. "Do you realize that is the third or fourth time you have spoken of such?"

"Is it? I'm sure you're mistaken." As though

the question was an uncomfortable one, he straightened and strode down the hallway with her still in his arms.

"I'm not. Several times you have uttered apologies for not being perfect. Now I would know—do you require perfection? In others as well as yourself?"

"Should we not strive toward such?"

"How can one seek such an impossible goal when to be human is to be imperfect? Is not the very perfection of man to learn about his own imperfections?"

She heard his intake of air, felt the hitch when his feet faltered. "Did you just quote at me? In *Latin*?"

She replayed the last sentence in her mind and realized she had. "Saint Augustine, I believe, of the Roman empire."

He resumed his confident pace with a chuckle. "I know full well who that was, having history drummed into me by more than one overeager instructor. I just didn't expect a mere slip of a woman to be quoting him at me."

"Because women cannot learn Latin?"

"Because most women are mute whenever I'm near. This holiday's been stranger than any other...with one startling revelation after another. Why not let it continue?" he said cryptically. "Go on, quote at me all you like."

She scoured her mind for another appropriate quotation, unwilling to disappoint the challenge she heard in his tone. Scoured again yet came up empty. "A pox on you and your deuced goose, for you have thoroughly cooked mine! Anything else that comes to my lips is weaker than the last."

He perplexed her thoughts further when he hefted her higher and skimmed his lips over hers, still striding toward some unknown destination. "I owe you a berry."

What he owed her was a dose of common sense, that which he seemed to steal with but his presence.

"Take myself, for example," she said solemnly, determined to subdue the tingle racing across her mouth and return to the prior topic, which he hadn't taken as seriously as she needed him to. "Were I to hold myself up to the standard of perfection, I would fail ere I ever began."

"That's absurd."

"Is it, Lord Frostwood? Do you forget that an unseeing eye has failed at its intended design?"

"That's preposterous!" he shouted, shouldering past doors that thumped shut behind them. "To apply such nonsense to yourself. How can—"

"Shhh." She tugged sharply on the short strands of hair at his nape, hoping to quiet his outburst. "Perhaps, Sir Blusters About, instead of holding *yourself* accountable to such an unrealistic standard—"

"Unrealistic? I assure you—"

"And I assure *you*," she overrode his protest, intent on being heard, "that whatever less-than-perfect habits—*ahem*, giving orders, whistling whiskers through your teeth—you may possess, however few I'm sure they are, you would be a much happier and more pleasant person were you simply to strive toward being the best you can be, perfection aside."

He grunted and set her on her feet. "Are you insinuating I'm the opposite of pleasant? That I'm a veritable churl?"

"With me you have been all that is—dare I admit it?—charming and thoughtful." And delightfully forward, but she couldn't share that with him. "I only offer this token of my counsel based on the general comments that seem to flit about at the sound of your...your name. Stop! What are you—?"

Humming, he'd placed her right hand upon his shoulder. He grasped her left. "Preparing to dance. With you."

Sheer terror gripped Isabella and she stiffened. "You most certainly are not."

"Come now, there's no one here to see you dancing upon your ankle. We're alone and—"

She jerked away. "Is that where you brought me? To the ballroom?"

He attempted to gather her in his arms again and she evaded his efforts, darting several steps back. "Isabella? What causes your distress? Do you not wish to dance with me?"

She wished it with all her heart, but that mattered not.

Have you any idea the horrid spectacle you make of yourself? One of her father's tirades obliterated all reason. *And you question why I won't countenance a match for you? You're a disgrace and your unnatural contortions an abomination!*

Tepid as far as many of his refrains went but piercing all the same.

Now only one realization penetrated the

fear—Lord Frostwood could never see her that way. Never!

Having no idea where he'd placed her or how far into the room they'd come, or even the direction of the doors, she felt lost. Like a cornered animal, she lashed out at the person closest to her. "No! I most certainly do *not* wish to dance with you. Have I not declined every time you ask? And I wish you would keep your berries and your hands and *your lips* to yourself!"

A TRAINED guard dog attacked by a hissing kitten. That's the comparison that came to mind—and he was definitely the dog. A dog for baiting her so—but what had he done?

Frost was at a loss. Her sudden change in demeanor, the panic she couldn't hide...what precipitated it?

The idea that he was the direct cause seemed inconceivable given how well they meshed and talked upon any number of subjects—more freely than he'd ever conversed with any female. But something he'd done had struck a chord within her, hitting a very sour note indeed.

He infused a carefree note into his voice as he approached her with measured, sedate footfalls. "My berries, not to mention my lips and hands, feel significant sorrow at the thought of causing you grief and I will keep all three to myself henceforth."

"Lord Frostwood, nay! I did not mean it... not any of it." She ducked her head and he took it as a sign.

He touched the back of one restless hand, which she flipped to grasp his.

"Tell me?" he dared softly, stroking his thumb across several fingers.

"My father..." She looked up and gave a watery smile. "I'm not permitted to dance, you see."

And oh, how much he did.

"Not allowed to venture outside much beyond the enclosed garden or...or... Well, any manner of things."

Without her expounding further he could imagine. The idea of this spirited, vibrant woman locked away baffled him completely. Moving at a slumbering snail's pace, he lifted her hand to his lips, lingered there a moment. "That's two berries now."

"As if I'm expected to maintain an accounting when your bachelor's fare makes me all totty-headed."

At that rejoinder, he reached into his pocket and withdrew everything he could coil his fingers around. "Here. Take the lot of them."

He thrust several berries into her hand, most of which dropped to the floor before she could capture them because he captured her lips in a violent kiss. He could do no less at the admission his touch affected her as hers did him.

Attempting to kiss away the fear he'd just witnessed, Frost used his lips and tongue to speak for him, plying her with every ounce of comfort he could even as he availed himself of every ounce of passion she was willing to relinquish. Rash perhaps, kissing one such as her as he would a paid doxy—not that Frost ever dallied with doxies; maintaining a past mistress or two had always sufficed—but nothing sufficed now except possessing her lips. Almost brutally, despite how he tried to show restraint, but wishing he could banish every dilemma this delightful woman had ever faced and ever would.

When she moaned in her throat, Frost

started to pull back. But no, she only angled her head, exposing her neck, and murmured, "Here too?"

And he was lost. His mouth swooped toward the delicate skin she offered and his hands slipped past her shoulders to her spine and down...down...

Until he was molding the firm halves of her bum, kneading the supple flesh with his fingers while his tongue delved toward the sensitive spot at the side of her jaw, beneath one ear.

"Tell me to stop." His words were ragged.

She remained silent and his hands slid over the mounds of her arse, his debauched fingers aching to tug her long dress up and out of the way so they could touch bare skin, could feel the heat he already sensed emanating from between her clenched thighs. The heat that beckoned him onward as nothing in his life ever had.

"By God, Issybelle, tell me to stop!" This time it was a prayer, one uttered with every bit of passion he felt.

But he kept on kissing her, his lips unerringly finding hers when she only whimpered, "Never."

He dug his nails into her petticoat-and-skirt-protected arse to keep from doing anything more that he shouldn't and begged against her mouth, "I... I... I need you..." *to tell me to stop*, damn it, "God, how I need you, Issybel—"

The touch of her tongue halted his rambling plea.

The flesh beneath his fingers tensed and lifted as she came up on her toes and coiled her arms around his neck. Her tongue skimmed tentatively over his lips and then inside his mouth. He heard her breath catch. But maybe that was his because as she rubbed her tongue along his, she tightened her arms, bringing their chests into contact.

The swell of her breasts branded him.

His fingers flexed again on their delightful handfuls and he sucked harder than he meant to on her tongue, all in an effort to keep from raising those skirts, from ripping that modest neckline down, and from plunging his tongue and his body where neither had any right to be.

Not now. Not when he'd yet to state his intentions. Or decide precisely what they were.

Her untried kisses and hesitantly bold responses told the truth—she'd never taken a lover, and Frost wasn't so far gone he'd steal her innocence.

If a dalliance was all he wanted, there were no doubt other, more experienced females present or wenches available in the nearest village willing to accommodate his ardor.

But he feared the Latin-quoting, dancing miss in his arms had ruined him. He feared no one else would do.

And he feared he might expire from oxygen neglect if he didn't remember to breathe.

Groaning with the effort, Frost gentled his sucking motions, forced his hands to unclench. Told his chest to forget the imprint of her breasts and went back to nuzzling her lips...her jaw...

And damned if he didn't find himself dipping past the neckline of her gown and his lips pressed between the shadowed cleavage before he'd ever thought to take in air.

Her fingers weaved through his hair, and he felt her mouth grazing against his bent head as she deposited wispy kisses wherever she could reach. He thought he heard her sigh "*Frost*", a tiny benediction, as she stood tall and

tendered her body and breasts up to his lasciv-
ious attentions.

Nay. Not yet. Not like this, some honorable
part of him clamored. *Not standing in a ballroom.* Not when he longed to explore her every
curve at his leisure, in the privacy of his own
bed. In the privacy of his own home.

His own home? So it seemed he did know
what his intentions were.

Her restless fingers plucked at his ears
when he stopped moving. And Frost realized
his tongue had sought and found a beaded
nipple.

Nay!

Dangerous kisses, these were, the ones
they couldn't seem to stop giving each other.
Dangerous to his formerly withdrawn existence. Dangerous to her virtue. Definitely dangerous to his elephant trunk of a nose.

He eased back, his tongue reluctantly re-
linquishing its prize. When he looked at her,
he saw tears brimming in her eyes. Wasn't sure
if his rascally hide was the cause or the cure.
"Slap my face if you're of a mind to."

She blushed and shook her head. "Never."

Now she blushed?

He straightened her dress, relieved to note

he'd not exposed anything more than the luscious upper swells. Which were reddened from his stubble, by damn. "Tell me, Miss Issybelle..." Was that his voice shaking like a choir boy's? He cleared his throat. "Are you this enticing to all of your suitors?"

"I wouldn't know. Father always forbade— *Suitors?* Does your query imply...?"

"I do believe it must." He couldn't mean anything else. Isabella wasn't the type of woman one toyed with, and he'd made up his mind to have her in his bed. Might as well do it right. "Well? Can I confidently assume a slap isn't coming my way now that I have stated my intentions?"

After dashing the semblance of moisture from her eyes, she slowly raised her hand to his jaw. His lips still throbbed. Blood pounded through his hands—and sundry other parts of his anatomy. But he forced himself to remain still as her gentle touch met his chin and drifted higher.

"I wish I could see you and consider your countenance for myself. Could see whether you dally with me most cruelly."

As her fingers crossed his mouth just then, he could no more offer the retort that rose to his tongue than abandon his efforts at wooing this delightful creature.

Too soon she whisked her hand away and tapped his temple, saying as if she believed not a word of his near declaration, "I think the kissing bough and Christmas spirit have addled your wits. Those sticky berries you ply me with have gummed up your garret."

"Likely so, but I assure you my intentions are of the purest." Though his desires were anything but.

She took her hand away and left him bereft. As though resolved, she said emphatically, "You cannot possibly be as handsome as Harriet would have me believe."

"Can I not? Noble nose aside, I am accounted to cut quite a dash."

She giggled at his audacity. "For shame, Lord Frostwood. You are entirely lacking in modesty."

"Then is that not another foible you can lay at my feet? Another instance of imperfection? Does that not please you mightily?"

At his good humor in mocking himself, hers seemed to evaporate. "No, for were *I* perfect I would see you and know for myself."

8

FRIENDSHIPS AMIDST FESTIVITIES

"WHAT HAPPENED TO YOUR GOVERNESS?" Isabella wondered aloud the next time Harriet latched herself to Isabella's side, during what was supposed to be a "restful afternoon repast".

But who could rest when the world marched on around them, in all its exciting vibrancy? So instead, the pair had relocated to Anne's private morning room, thus avoiding other guests while also avoiding being cooped up in their chambers.

"Primmy?" Harri had nicknamed Miss

Primrose thus, cackling over the similarities to their Regent's epithet, Prinny.

Isabella couldn't help but smile. "Aye. Miss Primrose."

With the advent of so many guests clustered within only a day or two, at meeting nigh on a hundred new people, trying to remember something about each so as to have any hope of recalling them again when next they crossed paths, she had quite misplaced her awareness of Miss Primrose.

She hadn't heard the other woman in a couple of days, and now that she thought about it, Harriet had been by her side much of that time as well. "What have you done with her?"

"She left a note for you. It's in my room," Harriet said. "I just remembered. Told me I could read it to you unless you wanted my sister to—but I am certain I would do a better job of it. I shall retrieve it for you later, after I rehearse my recitation—"

"Harriet Antoinette Larchmont!"

"Mama." Harriet shuffled to standing. "When did you get here?"

"Never you mind that. Be off with you now, girl, for retrieving Lady Isabella's letter is the *best* thing you can do, ere I send you outside to sleep in the stables." Lady Ballenger, Harriet's mother, cried, sitting next to Isabella with an exasperated huff. "Please forgive my youngest, Isabella. I would like to claim she tries, but, in all honesty, one must wonder—"

"The stables?" Glee shone from Harriet's tone. "*Truly?* You would let me sleep—"

"Upstairs! Show some consideration and pen your own missive *to me*: I want four hundred words on why *self-absorption* is a sin best avoided. Before dinner, young lady."

"Four *hundred*? Whatever will I write—"

"*Six* hundred!"

Which was enough motivation to send Harriet scurrying audibly out of the room. "That was an impressive feat, Lady Ballenger," Isabella complimented. "How long have you been assigning missives as punishment?"

"Since the ever-persevering Miss Primrose suggested it as a successful measure. The pen might be mightier than the sword, but in Harriet's case, her tongue thinks it's mightier than both." Another huff. "I aim to teach her differently before she leaves the shielding bosom of our family to start her own."

After confirming Isabella was fine on her

own, Lady Ballenger scuttled off to tend other guests. Leaving Isabella to her recollections of the brief time spent with the letter-assigning governess.

Isabella had shared several quiet conversations with the equally quiet, if thoughtful, young woman since she'd arrived. One in particular had brought a calm sort of joy for all its unusualness...its normality.

Taking pleasure in an unexpectedly warm afternoon shortly after she'd come to Redford Manor, both women had found themselves outside, under parasols, listening to Harriet shriek and play with some critter or another.

"I confess," Miss Primrose had ventured after a few moments' cursory discussion of the weather and Harriet's exuberance, "other than a cherished, aged friend of my uncle's, I have not been around a blind person. Pardon my blunt speaking. I realize I am naught but a servant here, but if there anything I can do to assist you, you have but to ask."

"Would you— Do you mind..."

"Anything, Lady Isabella. For the Larchmont family are all vocal and powerful forces to be reckoned with. Those of us with a more, shall I say, reserved nature, might have a ten-dency to feel all at sea."

Exactly. Even with Anne's consideration and Harriet's desire to please at every turn, for someone used to the solitude of their own company and little else, it was, at times, enough to make one feel rather adrift. "'Tis as-tute of you to notice. And I would be very grateful should you describe your features, if that is not overly forward of me to request."

"Not at all." Miss Primrose's voice took on a lighter note. "Although I am surprised Harriet would not have already regaled you with my appearance and her criticisms of such."

"Criticisms?" Tightening her hold upon her parasol, Isabella turned toward the voice beside her. "I cannot imagine Harriet would venture an intentionally harsh word—"

"All in fun, I assure you. Forgive me if I indi-cated otherwise. But I do have a tendency, out-side of our lessons and time together, to keep to myself. And Harriet is forever complaining that I do not wear colors 'becoming to my complex-ion'." Her companion gave a laugh. "As though it matters much what a governess wears."

"Did you know, until Anne appropriated a

lady's maid for me, I never knew whether my stockings were suitably coordinated to my gown, much less each other." She lifted her skirt a few inches and pointed one foot. Then the other. "What say you? Am I coordinating today?"

"Exquisitely," Miss Primrose confirmed. "As to myself, I confess I do dress rather somberly. Usually in browns. Simply because they don't show dirt as much as lighter colors and it does help one stay in the shade, as opposed to drawing attention to oneself. I cringe every time the beautifully attired Harriet gets mud or dust or animal dander—or, heaven forfend, squitters—about her person and upon her pale dresses. For one so gently bred, she does so like to gambol about with the livestock and stable inhabitants."

Squitter. That was a new one to add to her collection.

"I believe my features are rather plain," Miss Primrose continued, "nondescript, if you will, but I boast vibrant hair that resembles cooked carrots more than one might wish"— that brought a smile—"that I keep tightly pulled back—the better to hide its unfortunate color. Brown eyes, a countable number of freckles across my nose, hence the parasol, and a bigger bosom than one in my position might wish. How is that?"

"Smashing." Isabella laughed. "I can picture you so much more clearly now, for the tone of your voice and lilt of your words as you spoke helped paint a picture every bit as much as what you said. Thank you."

Another squeal from Harriet. Another honk—from a goose?—sounded from the green in front of them. "How difficult is it to keep her focused on lessons?"

"Lady Harriet? You have no inkling of the difficulty therein. I gather I came after a number of governesses who quite gave up schooling her at all."

"But you have persisted?"

"I simply had to out-determine her, and identify what might entice her attention where I needed it, if only for a short duration."

"Frolicking with her four-legged associates?"

"That and the occasional two-legged one. She's taken to making friends with a couple of the swans over at her home. Being here, with the extended visit to her sister and Lord Redford? It's brought about an entirely new realm of beasts for her to befriend. What of yourself? Have you a pet back home?"

As if her father would allow such a thing. "Nay. One reason it has been a delight, sneaking a few purrs and pets from Anne's Beatrice."

"Count yourself among the few, then. For her cat usually keeps out of sight of any but her and Lord Redford." Miss Primrose lowered her voice. "Shall I let you in on another secret?"

"Only if you're of a mind."

"That cherished friend of my uncle's? The blind one?"

"Aye?"

"He's a dog."

Isabella giggled.

"Named Mercury."

"After the planet?"

"Not at all. After the Roman god, protector of thieves."

"Mercury, the cherished friend, is a conveyancer?"

"Oh, is he! Because blind or not, that canine has the ability to steal trinkets right and left."

. . . . .

"WHAT DID you think I might have done with her?" Harriet asked now, plopping down on the settee next to Isabella, and the pleasurable memory wafted back into its box. "Locked my governess in the dungeon?"

"Redford Manor has a dungeon?"

"Stranded her out in the folly? Left bread-crumbs, so the hermit could find his way to her—"

"Harriet." That was Anne, under her breath as she came back into the room. Just the one word.

But it proved effective enough. "Oh, very well. Truth be told, she's on holiday—from me! Much like Beatrice took her own holiday from the guests and ensuing melee."

"Ensuing melee? You're quoting your mother again."

"I am. She told Anne..." Harriet's voice rose in pitch. "'When the *horde* starts to descend, send your pet to *Papa*. Bea will either hide in your old bedchamber, corner mice in the kitchen, or cuddle up with his gout-ridden self. Either way, better there than here, *scampering* from room to room, trying to avoid guests and *evade*'—still quoting, mind—'Harri's latest feathered fascination.' No more quotes. Have you met him? My—"

"Enough, Harri." Anne cupped Isabella's hands around a warm glass. "Go trouble someone else with your poultry prattle. Issy-bee's ears are tired."

"Are they?" Harriet demanded. "Oh, here is your letter."

"Only a bit," Isabella said on a smile, feeling not only the folded square slipped between her fingertips, but also the warmth of not just the beverage—spiced, heated wine or wassail, if the scents drifting up toward her nose were to judge by—but of the company, the joy of the season. The surprising peace and wonder that being around these beautiful people created in her soul.

And if one particular beautiful person brightened her soul even more, on these cold and chilly days? Well, she would continue to store up every second of his vibrant presence, every minute and memory she could, store them away in that small box near her heart so she would never feel cold and lonely again.

AND SO THE magical holiday continued...

With Lord Frostwood squiring her about for two more days *in* his arms—"While your ankle comes up to snuff"—then for several more *on* his arm—while he scowled at Simon Gregory and any other man who dared approach her. (Both Harriet and Anne made sure to inform Isabella of this repeated occurrence.)

With Lord Frostwood partnering her at most of the holiday amusements.

With Lord Frostwood exchanging berries for kisses...

Oh, Isabella knew not to take his attentions to heart—she was simply convenient and he was simply bored. That had to be why he showered such consideration upon her.

But oh—his kisses.

As if he'd recognized the desperation she'd shown ardently responding to him in the ballroom, his kisses changed, became lighter and more playful. Definitely safer. But Isabella felt them no less intensely.

Whether the proper application of his lips upon her wrist above her glove or the wholly improper slide of his mouth upon the back of her neck just before he escorted her into the dining room—and she gasped loud enough to be heard in Scotland—or the soft press of his lips upon hers before he bid her good night...

Each of his kisses left her breathless and yearning for more. And clutching the latest berry he'd snuck into her hand.

At the rate they were proceeding, the kissing bough ought to be almost bare.

What would he do then?

What would she?

Especially since the days marched on toward Twelfth Night...

With her falling harder and harder for a man she'd never see.

———◦◦◦———

"MAY I JOIN YOU, LADY ISABELLA?" The soft voice preceded a brief touch to her shoulder. "'Tis Uriana Gregory, daughter of Lord and Lady Fairfax, who asks, if you did not already know by my noisy nose which has a wretched tendency to announce my presence before I can do so myself."

The unexpected introduction had Isabella scooting farther toward the side of the settee in the large drawing room where Anne had escorted her after nuncheon as the weather proved too cold and calamitous for the after-noon's planned sleigh rides.

With the crackling fire warming her from several feet beyond, Isabella gestured to the empty space beside her. "Please do, Miss Fair-fax. Er, Mrs....?"

The cushion dipped slightly when the other woman sat down. "Aye, 'tis Mrs. Gregory now. Something I am still gaining familiarity with."

"The name?"

"And being married, both."

"Ah..." Isabella found her gloved fingers fidgeting amongst themselves. "Which Mr. Gregory are you wedded to?" Not Simon, surely...

"Samuel. Who, I confess, is as uncomfort-able exchanging prattle with females as I am with men."

"But he—he..." How she hated being in the dark at times, unable to gauge expression. To know who might be close by. "Are we alone? Is anyone near enough to overhear us?"

"Quite alone. I gather Harriet has devised a play and is assigning parts—all the parts—to ladies present."

"Even the male roles?"

"And animal ones as well!"

That brought an unclenching of her fingers and a smile, for in the past, all roles had been portrayed by men. "That is very Harriet of her."

"A great number of fellows are watching the to-do in the ballroom, while a few others have gathered in here and look to be debating cards or billiards."

Isabella gathered courage. "Both Mr. Gregorys have been rather effusive in their compliments toward me. I did not... Did not realize either were married." But really, what did she know of how women her age and the men around them might go on? "Neither have I taken a word to heart. Oh, I do hope I did not offend."

"Not in the least. Flirt away with my Sam, if you're of a mind," the new Mrs. Gregory encouraged—and she sounded sincere. "You are only the *second* woman he's felt at sufficient ease to practice his skills on."

"Oh." Should she be flattered? Or insulted? "And the first?"

"Married him."

Flattered, then. Definitely flattered.

"Sam is not at all fond of large gatherings

—much like myself. When we arrived, I set him the task of practicing small talk and exchanging pleasantries. You are the unfortunate recipient, I gather. Likely chosen to needle Simon."

The two women shared a laugh. "And please, call me Ria, *Uriana* being rather an unfortunate choice I still blame my parents for. Shall I impart a confidence? If it isn't overly bold on such a short acquaintance?" Before Isabella could respond, touched that she seemed to inspire such trust and shared secrets from those she had met this holiday, Ria continued. "I am for*ever* being mistaken for my elder sisters. It can be disheartening, to not be recognized for oneself."

Sisters, plural. "Are you triplets? Quadruplets? Are there *more* of you?"

"Not unless father was naughtier than he ought to be. Nay, just the three of us. And all born individually. We claim two and four years between us. However, we look much the same, sound and sneeze much the same, and are continually confused for each other—and that, by people who can *see*. I cannot imagine how much difficulty you must be having, trying to discern people's identities by voice alone."

How refreshing. For she was the second person to broach the subject of Isabella's blindness so openly, not at all with the furtive shame Father always tried to make her feel. "'Tis not only voice. Sometimes it's the way someone treads, the sound of their shoes and how fast or slow they walk, how their weight settles upon the floor or in a nearby chair. They might have a pleasant—or peculiar— scent specific only to them. Some laugh loudly, some softly—"

"And some laugh not at all."

"Aye! So you see, there is much more I lean on than just how someone's voice may sound."

"Utterly fascinating. Truly. Harriet mentioned you reside at the Spierton estate? I reside not overly far from there, and as we have now been introduced, would you be amenable should I call on you there, to further our association, should you desire one?"

As if Father would allow that.

But Isabella refused to think of such horrid unpleasantness today. Easier to pretend the freedom of the season would continue than face what she knew would come after she returned home. At least until she was sent off according to Father's whims.

"By all means. I would love to receive you." Not that she would ever be given the chance. "To learn more about you. Your likes and interests. Whether you take milk in your tea or sugar in your chocolate. I'll confess my own secret, shall I? I—" Unused to revealing emotional intimacies with anyone but Anne, not counting a certain lord who made her feel all sorts of heat and disharmony both, Isabella wasn't about to bare her deepest self on such a short acquaintance. But neither did she want to remain aloof or alone.

Drumming one restless hand upon the flat of the settee, she confided, "I have not ventured beyond my father's estate of late." Not for years and years. "Being here, sharing conversations, it is much as though I inhabit a new world."

"*Aaa-chooo!* Pardon me." It sounded as though Ria riffled through her reticule or person until finding a kerchief. "Being in society brings its own trials to me and my sisters as well. Fragrances, you see, we are dreadfully —" A sniffled snort, a gentle blow. Another two sneezes. "Dreadfully responsive to them."

"Perfumes and the like? How awful."

"One would think. But nay, you get used to doing without when you feel so much better. Our home eschews greenery of any sort, flowers, the perfumes you mentioned, and it has become somewhat of a safe haven. But if one never ventures out—"

"Then one misses out."

"Exactly!"

After a few moments more of congenial conversation, her new fumbled about, sniffed twice—unnecessarily, it sounded—and then, "May I... " Ria's voice lowered to a whisper. "May I prevail upon you to do a favor for me? I had not thought to prey upon you thus, but it occurs, now that we have chatted, that you could help me solve a puzzle. "

"Me? Certainly. If it is within my ability." Though Isabella doubted what manner of favor *she* could bestow.

"Could you, perchance, simply ask Lady Redford..."

"Ask her what?"

"Who in the blazes is Lord Grayson?"

Whereupon, Ria shared a vastly amusing tale of *her* whereabouts during part of Edward and Anne's betrothal ball, some two years prior...

The story that followed, told in hushed tones that put Isabella in mind of furtive glances and surreptitious mysteries brought forth such gales of laughter no less than three others interrupted to inquire what was so humorous, only to be sent on their way no wiser than they were before.

"I say—" Isabella's breath caught. Her sides hurt. Cheeks ached. Stomach threatened to cramp. 'Twas glorious! "I say, Ria, if it were anyone else, I would not believe a word. But your version of the incident, told from quite the different direction I will allow, speaks only truth, for it corresponds with what Anne shared. Though without the element of jollity, I admit. Aye, I may know the answer you seek, but let me assure myself of its accuracy, when no one else is around."

"And without alluding to my presence?"

"Definitely. No need to confound the mother-to-be."

ACROSS THE ROOM, two men observed the pair of amused females.

One with the pleasant serenity of a host well satisfied, secure in the knowledge that those welcomed into his home were pleased with the party and company his dear wife had arranged; the other with the indulgent smile of a man well satisfied, watching the woman who commanded his interest relax sufficiently to laugh loud and long, tickling his own mirth though he knew not what caused hers.

"I see your Isabella is conversing with Anne's Intelligent Blonde Friend."

His Isabella? Would that she could be his. Frost let the claim pass without comment. "One of the stuffy-headed Fairfax chits?"

"Amelia? Virginia? They're hard to tell apart." Ed pointed to another corner of the large room, where several men had set up a couple of card tables. "The youngest one married Sam Gregory, did you know?"

Gregory.

The name was enough to turn Frost's stomach sour. Which was absurd. Before this week, he had held both Samuel and Simon in high regard. Had jealousy sullied his judgment? "I wonder what Saint Augustine would say about that?"

"What?"

"Jealousy," Frost muttered without thinking, his gaze drawn again to the laughing women.

"Oh-ho! If that is where you veer, and after so few days, I see you heading straight up the altar and soon. Anne will be—"

"Stubble it."

"Although... He who is jealous is not in love."

The uncharacteristic words from Ed whipped Frost's attention away from Isabella. He narrowed his eyes, attempted to soften his rigid posture without success, and waited.

"Saint Augustine." Ed's gaze held more gloat than warranted. "You wanted to know what he thought of jealousy. Just so happens I caught Miss Primrose and Harriet having a lesson on ancient philosophers and theologians last week."

"I daresay it wasn't in Latin."

"Nay, in the King's English, it was."

He who is jealous is not in love.

Bah.

He wasn't jealous. And he refused to be in love.

So with a fierce frown—that Ed only laughed at—Frost strode determinedly toward the card players. He would join in and be civil to both Sam and Simon if it martyred him.

"So you see," Ria concluded, "not only am I forever being mistaken for one of my sisters, sometimes I fail to be recognized at all—even erroneously."

It took a long time for the chuckles to subside. When they did, Isabella decided to risk an important query of her own.

"What can you tell me of Lord Warrick? For you would have met him that night." Isabella had overheard conversations between Lord Frostwood and Edward, touching upon the absence and plight of their friend. Her two inquiries, posed to Lord Frostwood, about the war experiences between the three men had been met with curt answers and a swift turn of topic—which had done nothing to assuage her growing curiosity.

"Only formally," Ria said. "When he was introduced to me, along with several others. He's too handsome and far too confident for me to engage in repartee. I did not speak with him or Lord Frostwood at all. Amelia engaged with them both for an entire set, said Lord Warrick was outrageous and amusing and drew people to him like horses to a hay barn. Too practiced to be authentic, she said."

"What do you mean by that? I know only that he was paralyzed and aspires to walk again, and that his presence is missed."

"No one so grievously injured could be that jovial so soon after. For his sake, I pray he recovers the use of his legs. Or the acceptance of their loss."

"And your sister Amelia, has she set her cap for anyone?"

"There is one gentleman I believe she fancies."

"Is he in attendance? I am sure Anne would—"

"As to that, I cannot say."

"Because you do not know?"

"Because just as I trust you will not betray me to Lady Redford, I will not—"

"Betray your sister. You are to be commended. I should not have inquired."

"I am glad you did. Both my sisters are at ease in company. It is a relief to find a female friend of my own who isn't jabbering merrily away with ten others."

"It is overly difficult to follow so many conversations at once."

"And with your two beaus, I gather—"

"*Two* beaus?"

"Lady Isabella, it is clear to anyone who pays attention that both Simon and Lord Frostwood vie for your companionship."

"I— He..." Isabella mashed her lips together, uncertain how to respond.

"For myself, I have observed the man your affection favors."

"Mr. Gregory—meaning *Simon*, not your Samuel—has been more eager with his attention than one might expect on so short an acquaintance." Or at least that was how it seemed to Isabella. "Surely, he will not be wounded by..."

"Your predilection for another?" A gloved hand met her own in a gentle squeeze. "Think nothing of it. Simon stays cooped up with his experiments far too much. When he does tear himself away and attend an event such as this, I think he embraces every aspect without reservation. Make no mistake, the week after Twelfth Night, he'll likely be locked away with his safety tubes and crucibles, powders and ignition sources, making all manner of noise and mess, sparing not a thought to anyone here."

Relief lightened Isabella's being. "Does *your* Mr. Gregory have equitable scientific leanings?"

Another snort, but this one from laughter as Ria released her hand, gasped and chuckled her way through another sneeze or two before answering. "Gracious no. The only science Sam is ever interested in is how many cakes and biscuits he can make before his scheduled precious weekend of drinking souses him beyond baking."

"Your husband...*bakes*?" Isabella had never heard the like, not from anyone of their station or that of well-off gentry, which she took both Gregory brothers to be. Certainly, there were celebrated French chefs (male ones), especially in London, but here in the country? A landed *husband* who dusted his hands with flour and willingly worked in the kitchen? And he did so *soused*? "I boggle with curiosity for more."

"Shhh." The other woman leaned in and Isabella caught a waft of the fresh scent of limes. "That really is mine and Sam's secret. I should not have revealed such."

"I vow, it will stay with me." A promise

easily kept, for Isabella knew how to maintain her own counsel. "I'm just... Dismayed. I doubt my father has ever stepped foot in the kitchens a single day of his life."

"My Bemused Baker. That's what I call my dear Sam. One would think *I* have just indulged in a weekend of revelry, the way I go on. You, Lady Isabella, are far too easy to confide in."

"Do you think it's because I cannot see? People assume—"

"Nothing of the sort." A quick blow, a single sniff, then, "My dear, you inspire confidences because you *listen*. That has nothing and everything to do with your sight, I am sure. For myself, my tongue tends to freeze in groups, and leave me mute or muttering. Speaking with you, one-on-one as we are, is something I have not done with anyone outside of my sisters. Thank you for one of the most delightful encounters I have had since fortunately chancing upon a like-minded spouse."

With a flurry of sneezes, snuffles and— what sounded like—smiles, Ria took herself off, but not before promising to visit Isabella, cakes and biscuits in hand, the next time her husband indulged in a bevy of bosky baking.

———————◦◦◦◦———————

BECAUSE SHE CAPTURED his interest as nothing else, the Earl of Frostwood observed the enticing Isabella most thoroughly. He noticed she tended to play least-in-sight when others were milling about and not yet settled. Saw how she maintained a high degree of dignity and an impressive semblance of independence.

But was she really? Independent?

He knew she'd been denied a dowry but beyond that she remained mute, insisting she'd rather not dredge up unpleasant reminders of life outside Redford Manor.

Questions poked at him like pointy leaves from a sprig of holly. She was too alluring not to have a harping mother or overprotective aunt nearby. Too young not to have a chaperone plastered to her side.

Too old to still be in the schoolroom.

Too ideal for his peace of mind.

It seemed to him that the days flew by with

the wretched speed of a swarm of locusts. Though he strove to hold tight to every magical moment, imprint every memory he could, they came at him so hard and so fast he could barely remain standing. And this, from the man who previously loathed Christmastime above every other season to be endured? It was unfathomable—how easily she made him see everything differently with naught but her presence.

Thank God for Ed. Ed *and* Lady Redford. Without them and their pestering invitation, where would he be now? Four bottles castaway with the headache and sour stomach and gut full of regret that came with it. Certainly no closer to the feeling of euphoria that drifted just within reach.

Because he found the more time he spent with Issybelle, the more he realized how very closed off he'd become from everything and everyone save a few choice friends, how very much he'd driven himself beyond perfection and into exhaustion. Recognized how she melted chinks in his crusty exterior, exposed the man beneath—a man who no longer thought of himself as cold, his heart a block of ice. As *Frost*.

With every hour he spent in her company,

he recalled more of the boy he'd been...Nicky. Christmas memories and blissful recollections of childhood besieged his mind for the first time in decades. And he allowed it. Allowed the reminders to bring comfort instead of pain.

Allowed himself to become *Nicholas*. And how he wanted the thawing to continue.

But time was running out.

His nose no longer resembled an elephant's; her palms had healed nicely.

Nicholas knew because he'd licked the left one just yesterday before opening the door to her bedchamber where Isabella persisted in retiring for her afternoon "restorative".

He also knew she always slipped back out of her room *after* hearing his footsteps retreat —something he'd determined one day when she didn't leave immediately as he loitered directly across the hall—and sped toward the ballroom using the most circuitous route imaginable. In order to avoid crossing paths with himself or anyone else, he surmised.

However efficiently she did so, she escaped as regularly as the tick of a clock, retreating to the empty ballroom to move in ways too magical to be termed "dance". She lifted his spirits with her fluid, elegant motions. With her lithe, alluring grace.

And that wasn't all she lifted either.

At some point Nicholas had come to realize he wanted her with a fervent desire that went beyond any he'd experienced with prior liaisons.

He wanted her body.

He wanted her spirit.

He wanted her *love*.

Blast it! He wanted her to be his countess and he had absolutely no idea how to go about securing such a thing.

Not when she was so deuced elusive about her last name, her parentage, her past. Certainly a single word in Ed's ear would have resolved the mystery to his satisfaction. But he'd been reluctant to do so, only wanting to hear about Isabella *from* Isabella.

Not when she didn't trust him sufficiently to agree to dance with him when he asked. Or to confess the truth about her afternoon lying-in, which was anything but. Not when she repeatedly accused him of being nothing more than a dangler, a rakeshame, interested in naught but a holiday dalliance.

It was time for a change in their circumstances.

Time to convince her of the sincerity of his regard.

Hell, she'd already changed him, Nicholas thought ruefully, barging past the heavy double doors and into the ballroom—wincing when his left hand hit the ornate wood harder than intended—humming a damn Christmas tune!

He'd begun enjoying the gaiety of the season again, enjoying life again, and it was thanks to an unassuming scrap of a woman he no longer wanted to live without.

And it was time she bloody well took him seriously.

9

ISABELLA—GASP!—REJECTS
A FESTIVE OFFER

───────◆◆◆───────

NICHOLAS MICHAEL HENRY WINTEN, Lord Frostwood.

Isabella Jane Winten...Countess of Frostwood.

Lovely ring to it, she thought, envisioning the wondrous future her daughter would have as his bride.

Nicholas...so roguishly handsome, even with that dour frown—the one he had difficulty holding on to when Issybelle was near, she'd noticed.

She also noted how he'd moderated his consumption of spirits after that first night. Most thoughtful of him—one certainly didn't want their future son-in-law to turn into a corned toss pot.

Aye, most thoughtful.

Even more so was how he forbore mocking her daughter for her most unusual pastime as Isabella's papa had been wont to do—disagreeable toad.

Also quite unlike the cur she'd been wedded to, when Nicholas barked a command, it was out of habit and a desire for order, not with the intent to feel superior or lord his station over others.

And Nicholas was an earl, Hervey a mere baron. Ha!

Ah yes, she'd be smiling nigh until the wedding. If only she had someone to share her joy with...

❧

"Lord Frostwood? Without doubt I have seen—dare I say it?—how *pleasant* he's become of late and have *you* noticed what an attachment he seems to have developed to Lady Isabella?"

"Why certainly. One would have to be blind to miss it." There was a slight snicker, instantly subdued. "Oh, I did not mean that, truly. She's a lovely girl but one who best take care ere she lose more than her heart."

"She was raised properly." That was Lady

Ballenger's voice, Harriet and Anne's mama. "Her mother saw to that."

"But with her mother gone, perhaps 'proper' behavior has fled as well? She does make herself absent from a number of events, you must admit."

Isabella paused on her way to the ballroom. By now she knew exactly when the musicians started their rehearsal and she'd easily excused herself from an afternoon of charades —a most difficult game, to be sure, when one had naught but the shouted guesses of others to base their own wild conjectures upon.

Winding through the great manor, she'd come upon Anne's mother and some of the other women in a side parlor, gossiping over tea and cakes—gossiping over *her* and *Lord Frostwood*.

They didn't know Isabella sufficiently to be concerned about her feelings. Well, perhaps Anne's mother did, but it had been a good many years since she'd seen the carefree Isabella who grew up romping with her daughter.

Hovering near the doorway, Isabella couldn't bring herself to continue on, not yet. She should've anticipated something like this...she chose to keep to herself more often than not and rarely joined in large, convivial conversations. When too many people spoke at once, it was simply too much to keep up with, identifying who said what and who was about to jump into the fray, to know when it would be appropriate to add whatever comment might be flitting through her mind.

Compounded by her solitary existence at Spierton, it only made sense she tended to seek the privacy of her own company or that of a cherished friend or two rather than actively participate in the larger assemblies. Especially given how the two women beyond Anne who made an effort to befriend Isabella were no longer in attendance, Miss Primrose leaving shortly after everyone else arrived, and Ria and Samuel Gregory departing several days ago to visit family. With Anne busy hosting all her guests, was it any surprise Isabella spent whatever magical moments remained with the man who *wanted* to spend his moments with her?

Justified or not, none of that made hearing comments about her life being bantered about so blithely any easier...though she was curious how others saw her, and how they might view her current association with Lord Frostwood.

Praying no one would cross her path in the hallway, Isabella pressed against the wall, pushed away the guilt, and listened with all her might.

"Lose more than her heart? You don't mean to imply she's light-heeled or free with her favors?"

Mistletoe berries aside, she wasn't...

"Oh, not at all. What I meant was everyone knows how he treated his mother all those years, consigning the poor woman to the country, *never* bringing her to London and never—"

"Never visiting her, not once," another voice finished in astonishment. "So cruel! So cold and heartless."

Someone else put in, "Well, I for one can hardly countenance his reputed treatment of her, not the way Lord and Lady Redford speak so highly of him."

"Be that as it may," the first voice again, "what shall we do about dear Isabella? We cannot let a green girl fall for a man who hasn't any feeling. It would be completely remiss of us."

"Unfeeling? How can you say that?" Anne's

mother queried. "Have you not seen the way he fixes himself to whichever corner of the room she's inhabiting, glowering at anyone who dares approach?"

Warmed at having that last bit confirmed, Isabella listened only a bit longer before moving on.

Hearing additional speculation wasn't necessary; what others thought didn't skew her own feelings toward Lord Frostwood in the least—for the man who spent time with her was anything but unfeeling.

Although their comments did make her doubly curious about his life outside of Redford Manor, and doubly certain she had no place in it.

———◦◦———

"YOU'RE LATE," he accused when she appeared at long last. "They have been practicing nigh on twenty minutes now."

Nicholas watched his words stop Isabella cold.

With every second that elapsed and the woman he'd expected failed to materialize, his agitation had surged, sinking his patience faster than eight stone tied to a goose feather.

After pulling wide every drape the cavernous room boasted—which hadn't done a damn bit of good, more winter clouds having rolled in—he'd paced the empty dance floor unceasingly.

The dismal sky and gloomy ballroom reinforced his grim mood. Even curdled the first taste of wassail he'd braved earlier, when hope held him in its thrall. By the time she eased through the doors, he was annoyed with her for concealing this part of herself from him and annoyed with himself for not confronting her sooner.

But she was here now, frozen just inside the double doors. And looking woefully uncertain.

"Nay, you are not hearing things."

Isabella opened her mouth, gave a little squeak, then clamped it shut. She hung her head, making no move to retreat or to explain.

He stood there, not ten feet away, and waited. For about two seconds then he blurted, "Aye, I know about your afternoon *restoratives*."

Nicholas heard how much venom the last word contained and hated that it bothered him so—her hiding from him. Hated more how easily such an occurrence never had to happen. "Why, Isabella? Why did you not tell me that initial day we conversed and you abandoned me for this that you needed to hear the musicians? That you needed to dance? Think you I would begrudge—"

"Please, Lord Frostwood. Please do not...do not..." She took several steps into the room and held out her hands beseechingly. "Please don't be angry with me. I know it's vulgar and despicable and I have no right to contort my limbs, no right..."

Now he was the silent one. Listening to her jabber on about her horrid actions and coarse demeanor and could he ever forgive her... On and on she implored, taking tiny, halting steps toward the area where he'd spoken from.

Having paced several strides to the left, she was far off the mark. It mattered not that she continued to reach out for him as she pleaded, mattered not that she should have been accusing *him* of spying on her, yelling at him for questioning her right to do anything she damn well pleased. For violating her trust and trapping her this way...

Nothing mattered except gaining an understanding of how the vivacious and confident woman he'd come to know had been transformed into an incomprehensible milk-and-water miss with nothing more than an irate sentence. One he had no right to even utter. "Isabella! Halt!"

She jerked as if struck then angled sharply until she faced him, her impassioned appeal trailing off.

He stood mute, struggling to comprehend the dichotomy with which they each viewed her actions.

Starkly...hesitantly, she queried, "Lord... Frostwood...are you still here?"

Propelled, he strode forward and gripped her shoulders. "'Lord Frostwood' be damned. Call me Nicholas. Call me an idiot, an imbecile or Lady Redford's favorite, a cork-brained simpleton. Call me anything you desire, sweetheart, but tell me why in the name of heaven would you think the sublime dance you engage in every afternoon could be considered vulgar? Then tell me you'll dance with me tonight. *With me*, by God."

She listed toward him. "What did you say?"

He tightened his hold on her, mentally cursing his bandaged left hand when it protested. "Are your lugs out now like your lamps? I spoke clearly enough. I want to know *why* you keep this beautiful, magical part of yourself from me. From the world. Why mask it at all? And why in blazes won't you dance with me?" His voice had roared to a crescendo.

Hers was a light breeze. "You...you don't think it's shameful?"

"Damn shameful I cannot hold you in my arms and waltz across the floor as I have dreamed for days. And nights—oh, the nights..."

She tried to tug away.

When he held firm, she turned her head to the side and he saw moisture dampening her lashes. He shook her to bring her head around. "*Why?*"

"Why do I behave like a heathen?" she fairly spat at him, going rigid beneath the grip of his hands. "Why do I contort my body in vulgar ways befitting a damn hedge whore?" He gasped at her language. Not so much stunned at hearing the words, but stunned at hearing *her* speak them—and in regard to herself. Before he could protest, she railed at him. "Or why do I hide from you? From everyone? Why won't I dance with you?

Is that what you demand to know?" Her body went slack, all the fight and flame drained from her. "Because I'm nothing but a wretched, damaged female whose only purpose in life is to draw in air that better belongs to another!"

With that, she wrenched from his slackened hold and jerked back only to round on him, breathing fire again. "Is that what you wanted to hear? What Father disciplines into my head every time he catches me moving in any manner he considers unbecoming—which means anything not sitting prim, back starched straight, hands folded, feet on the floor—and still as a grave—in a bloody chair!"

"Isabella..." he murmured, but she wasn't finished.

"Do you know he released my governess the moment the physicians told him my sight would never be normal? That the quote you so admired and everything else I have learned since is whatever Mama could bring to hand and share with me?" Her pale eyes flashed sparks at him. "That the first time Father caught me moving to music in my head he locked me in my room for three days so I could 'contemplate upon whatever reprehensible actions had drawn this particular punishment to me'? What else do you *demand* to know?"

She cocked her head and evaluated him in such a way he felt like a slimy insect about to be dissected. "Well? I'm sure there are thousands, no, make that *hundreds* more because ever since The Disastrous Accident he hasn't wanted to look upon his imperfect daughter and *orders* me from his sight any time I dare cross his path!"

Her tirade had drawn the attention of the musicians. They'd stopped playing and three of them were leaning over the balustrade. Nicholas waved them back. A gold sovereign or two should ensure their silence. He'd see to that after he saw to the mistaken woman trembling before him.

HER HEART BLED *a river of crimson; her wings ceased to sway. If she'd had air to breathe, it would've escaped on a sigh, one of despair.*

Not once since joining this dimension had hope and happiness seemed so unattainable.

She'd known of course, how he'd spurned their only child, first for daring to be female then with more vehemence once it became clear no male heirs would follow. Had known his anger increased once Isabella was no longer a "perfect" little lady to parade before any marriage-minded lords or their sons as a pawn for his political aspirations.

Had known his contempt raged stronger than compassion, his fury fiercer than love...

But knowing how her precious daughter had been treated and witnessing the effects with the clarity of one in the beyond were two vastly different experiences.

Oh, my darling... What has he done to you?

"Nicky'll take grand care of her, just see if he doesn't!"

Startled by the exuberant voice, she turned to behold an adorable golden-haired child. A beaming girl who'd joined her atop the lonely nimbus. "He calls her Issybelle too. Have you noticed? She's perfect for him, I think."

Yes, and I think he's perfect for her.

Marveling at the miracle she'd had no hand in, she extended one feathery wing. The child eagerly nestled beside her. "Are you not delighted?"

Most assuredly she was, beyond delighted in truth, for now she had someone to share her hope. "Aye, moppet, I do believe they are rather magnificently suited." As are we.

———————◦◦◦———————

So much became clear in an instant.

Why she'd chided him for aspiring to perfection.

Why she hid her love of dancing, though he still believed *that* particular word to be woefully inadequate for the splendor her limbs wrought.

Why she embraced his kisses—and dare he think *him* specifically—as she did, so uninhibitedly, so recklessly for one of her quality. So wonderfully. And as one set free for only a short time—with every expectation of being locked away again after a brief reprieve.

"No, no... You have it all wrong." He pulled her into his arms and hugged her tight, speaking over the sheen of glossy brown ringlets. "Vulgar? Nay! Issybelle, what you do is the most magical thing I have ever been blessed to witness. Why do you think I did not confront you that very first day? I could not speak for the lump in my throat clogged it with emotion unlike any I have ever experienced."

She stirred, and he embraced her more fiercely. "As for your father, whoever the rotter is, he deserves to be whipped—nay, *strangled*—for all he's done to harm you."

She leaned back as if to evaluate his countenance but instead gazed far beyond his shoulder. "You should not say such a thing—even in jest."

"Who says I'm jesting?" His fingers dug into her hips until her eyes flicked toward his. "It would give me great pleasure to destroy any man who would cause you such pain."

"Thank you."

"For what? Barging in and bullying you shamelessly?"

"For championing me wholeheartedly."

"Will you now tell me how in blazes you lost your sight? Your father isn't responsible, is he?"

"No, not at all." She peeled his hand free and he stoically refused to wince, finding solace when she turned in his arms until he stood cradling her backside along his front. Only then did she speak.

"It's difficult to discern...there was no notable event, no scorching fever or great blow, simply a swift lessening of my vision until it disappeared altogether. My eyes merely failed."

"They just...stopped seeing?"

"Mama first realized something was amiss when I began knocking into things. Spilling things." She heaved a sigh and he heard the guilt she'd heaped upon herself.

"The accident, you mentioned?"

Her head nodded beneath his chin. "Spilling things upon *important* people. I was a year or two younger than Harriet. Father had guests, several men whose favor he curried. I was carrying the tea tray—Mama allowed it after I begged, wanting to see these influential lords Papa spoke so highly of—when my foot snagged. I pitched forward and splashed hot tea all over Lord Wroxley, embarrassing Father to no end."

"You were but a child!"

He felt her slight shrug. "A child who by this time only saw small slices of what was before her and didn't realize it was anything unusual. Father accused me of crying false. When physicians confirmed my sight had narrowed and might soon be gone, he called me worthless because who wants a damaged bride likely to develop additional imperfections?"

"Oh, Issybelle, God no..." Her father was a buffoon's arse, and if he ever had the chance, Nicholas would extract immense satisfaction telling him so. For now, he told Isabella another truth. "Lord Wroxley's a whining wigsby, one who could stand a good dousing. I'm sure the tea did him— Wait." He swiveled Isabella around, his gaze seeking the old gash that spliced her eyebrow, that adorable, dangling curl obscuring the worst of it. "What about the scar on your forehead?"

"More of that stupid clumsiness I lay claim to, I'm afraid. I tripped over a pair of Father's boots and landed against a corner table." From all she'd told him—and all she hadn't—he'd wager the damn sod had left them there on purpose.

As a child when tragedy occurred, Nicholas had been in no position to offer protest or defend himself and vent his grief at the injustice. Now as a man with considerable influence and the power to have others do his bidding, he could no more take away her past pain or rectify the wrongs she'd suffered. But he could heal her heart as she was healing his.

Fisting his hands together so tightly he swore, Nicholas willed the useless anger to recede. Which it did in a trice for he had more significant feelings to address—hers. Uncoiling his fingers, he slid one beneath the ringlet and caressed the area above her right eye. "I'd thought this was to blame..."

Words failed him and he bent to press his lips to the spot.

"'Tis only an obvious reminder of my wretched clumsiness."

He growled, knowing instantly whose words she repeated. "Nay, never that." He moved his lips to her temple. "A mishap, 'tis all." To her cheek. "Something that simply happens without thought or plan." To the shell of her ear, causing her to fidget...so back to her cheek. "Not something one intends or ever needs to berate themself over again, just like my unforeseen blunder this afternoon."

Easier to share his own "wretched clumsiness" than to continue kissing and lose his head.

"Yours?"

"Aye." He held his left hand between them and brought hers to it so she could feel the wrapping. "Sliced a good inch along my palm earlier."

"Nicholas! Why did you not say something sooner? Has it been stitched?"

He smiled at her concern. "After spending years serving king and country and seeing all manner of wounds, I can assure you 'tis nothing that a bit of time and clean dressings won't heal."

Her fingers were gently frantic upon his hand. "You do not bam me? It truly isn't serious?"

"How could you think I lie?"

Her ministrations faltered, head lifted toward his. She cocked one eyebrow and pursed her lips. "Ahem."

He coughed self-consciously. "Well yes...I take your point, but did I not already confess I am the modicum of truthfulness everywhere but around...ah..."

"Me?"

He coughed again. "Peck my eyes with a deuced goose if I do not tell the truth. Now and forevermore."

"And what truth is that?"

"That no one ever muddled my mouth as you do. That I *want* to be muddled forever and —blast it—though it grieves me to no end, I know I need to speak with your father before I offer—"

"No." She covered his lips with her hand. Well, first his chin *then* his lips. "You must not speak thus. My course is set after Twelfth Night and does not—"

"With another?" he mumbled against her fingers. "Have you plans with another?"

"Nay. But what you speak now... Leave off spinning castles betwixt us, if you please. Come now, we have two nights remaining of this glorious holiday. Let us not mar it with talk of anything else."

He licked her fingers and she removed them at once. "Even when it is our future happiness I speak of?"

"Oh, Nicholas..."

"I shall change your mind and claim your hand, of that I promise you." Before she could protest further he added, "And *you* will promise me a dance."

"Will I now?" She gave a saucy tilt that sent those enticing ringlets bouncing. "Orders who?"

10

NICHOLAS COMMANDS A FESTIVE ENDING

———◆◆◆———

BLAST AND DAMN, the vexing chit still refused to dance with him.

I do not know how to waltz. Everyone will be watching... Oh, I just cannot! Please understand!

He understood one thing with surety. She *would* be dancing with him—and in mere minutes—and she wouldn't be concerned with where anyone else was directing their gaze either.

———◆◆◆———

JANUARY 5TH, 1814 ~ TWELFTH NIGHT

"As TOMORROW MARKS the end of our time together—" A chorus of good-natured boos interrupted Anne's statement. She made consoling noises until the clamor died down. "It has been a splendid holiday, has it not? And tonight, it promises to only get better."

From her seat near the corner, Isabella spared not a thought to what was in store, too embroiled in her own turbulent musings.

What Nicholas alluded to—a future between them—was all she'd ever dreamed of, more than she'd dared conceive, but Father would never agree to her marrying a peer. To her marrying anyone. For it equated to advertising her defects. He'd never allow it and, as a female, she had no right to gainsay him. No authority to do as Nicholas decreed.

And she must stop thinking of him as such! He was *Lord* Frostwood.

Oh, but how it hurt to deny him and her own heart.

You don't have to, some rebellious imp whispered. The same imp she suspected who had encouraged her to come to Redford Manor. The same imp who kept urging her to admit to Nicholas how she felt. But how could she? They were from different worlds, different—

"Because..." Anne's voice rang out, louder than before. "Everyone will be blindfolded for the duration of the evening!"

Blindfolded?

Pardon?

Excited murmurs erupted throughout the crowded ballroom. "Not the men of course—they need to know where they're going so they can lead, but all ladies will have their eyes covered. A truly *masked* ball, if you will." Anne clapped her hands. "Silk scarves are being distributed by the servants. Once yours is on—"

A butter-soft sash was thrust into Isabella's restless fingers. "But I'm not—"

"Yes, miss. Lady Redford said specifically you was to have one," the servant told her before departing.

"Each dance will be *gentleman's* choice," Anne continued. "Are you ready, ladies? Gentlemen, snare your partners."

Amid giggles and titters and the shuffling of many feet, Isabella sat there bewildered and baffled and *not* blindfolded. What was Anne about now?

"Come now," said a velvety-smooth voice from behind her just as the sash was snatched away. "You must do as your hostess instructs."

"Musicians...begin!"

As the first notes of a lovely, slow waltz commenced, fabric was stretched tight across her eyes and wrapped snugly about her head. "This was your idea, was it not?" she accused. "Do not answer. I know that it was."

Isabella started to fight him when he fashioned the knot. Started to, but chose instead to sit compliantly and offer only a token protest. "This is absurd. I cannot see anything as it is." For though anxious, she desperately wanted to know where this might lead.

With Nicholas taking her hand, pulling her to her feet and leading her onto the dance floor. That's where.

"Very necessary," he intoned, replicating their positions from a couple days prior. Only this time when he took her in his arms, she willed the instinctive fear to recede. There was no cause for alarm. She was in a ballroom where one was *expected* to dance, at a private house party no less and—perhaps most importantly of all—for once in her life, every other female was blinded too.

What an odd circumstance he'd created on her behalf. Isabella wasn't sure what to make of it.

"Don't hold yourself so stiffly," he ordered, and she caught the hint of cloves on his breath.

"Been sampling the wassail again?" her lips asked while her mind battled conflicting desires—staying put or wrenching away. And finding a place to hide.

"That I have." Giving her no chance for escape, he firmed his grip at her waist and around her hand and they were off. "It's every bit as delicious as I remembered."

Though her upper body remained rigid within the unfamiliar waltzing hold, her feet felt at home and she concentrated only on Nicholas, his strength, and his silent direction. Concentrated on *Lord Frostwood*, her stubborn conscience reminded.

After a single stumble, her legs stretched instinctively to match his longer strides and Isabella soon found herself soaring backward across the dance floor.

Not once did he clomp upon her toes. Not once did she allow any old refrains to mar her joy.

She was...dancing. Actually dancing!

Dancing *with* Lord Frostwood while other couples swirled about—she heard the rustle of long, fancy dresses circling nearby and the low murmur of conversations ebbing and flowing as she and her partner glided across the ball-room as graceful as swans on a lake... And she was part of it all thanks to this wonderful, magical man. Christmastime had never been so marvelous.

Eventually the music slowed and Anne instructed everyone to exchange partners.

Their feet waned to a stop and a dip of fear tumbled through her belly.

"Lady Isabella?" Simon Gregory queried. "Will—"

"Will be dancing with me for the duration." To emphasize, Lord Frostwood pulled her closer. His possession warmed her and calmed the knot of nerves—but it wasn't done. She *couldn't* dance with him and only him. It would be tantamount to an announcement.

It simply wasn't done! What else wasn't done was the objection Isabella knew she should offer but chose not to. In the lengthening silence, her eyelashes flickered strangely against the foreign sash.

"Very well, but be advised I may ask again," Mr. Gregory graciously acceded.

The music started yet Lord Frostwood remained in place. "Then I shall be forced to deny your request again. And again. Isabella will only be partnering me tonight and I her. Special circumstances, you know. Future wife and all."

Isabella gasped but the sound was covered by Mr. Gregory's cough. "Thought that might be the way of it. May I wish you both happy, then?"

"You may." Not a moment later he guided her backward, taking up the one-two-three rhythm.

"My lord?"

"Call me Nicholas, darling Issybelle. Future husband and all."

She laughed with a combination of sheer amazement and pure panic. "When Anne pronounced you an imbecile, I didn't realize she had the right of it. You cannot claim we are to be wed!"

"Oh? Thought I just did."

"It's terribly forward of you."

He hummed a tune nowhere near the waltz the musicians played and spun her in a fast circle. "Most likely."

"As were all your kisses."

"But you like my forward kisses."

"So I do, but Father will *never*—"

"You have an unreasonable fear of your father, have you considered that?" He spun her again.

An unreasonable fear. What a simple, succinct way to describe the emotions that roiled through her at the mere mention of the man.

"That's understandable." Nicholas stroked his thumb over her fingers, clasped her hand snugly and swung her the opposite direction. "As a boy, I suffered an unreasonable fear of my mother. I'll tell you about it sometime, but for now, do not forget that you, my dear, are a grown woman, one eminently capable of making her own decisions."

"A ruined woman," she retorted, her head, impossibly, more topsy-turvy than her feet, "practically on the shelf where I am expected to stay."

"You're so far from the shelf you aren't even in the same room." He faltered mid-spin. "Did you say *ruined*? Has some dastard taken advantage of you, Isa—"

"*Besides* you?"

That stopped him short. But not for long. With a deep chuckle, he was off again, twirling her about the floor with long sweeping strides she doubted had anything to do with the

proper steps of the waltz. "Those were or-
dained Christmas kisses I'll have you know,
Issybelle. I was commanded by tradition and
moved by the holiday spirit."

"Aye, and I was moved by your lips," she
confessed, holding tight to him and reveling in
the whirling sensation that overtook her. Between their conversation and his magnificent
dancing spins, dizziness made her careless.
"But now I'm to be *removed* to one of Father's
northern properties."

"Removed? Like a side of uneaten veal?"

"He's remarrying come February and in-
stalling his new bride at home."

The spins ground to a halt. Anger raged
from his voice and his tensed posture. "*What?*
And the sod's *evicting* you?"

"I'm an embarrassment to him, you see. I
fear I would be to you as well." She attempted
to tug free. He wouldn't allow her retreat.

"Embarrassment? To *me*? How could you
think—?" He leaned close and hissed, "Do you
think Ed is an embarrassment to his lady
wife?"

"Edward? Whatever do you mean?"

His voice turned cold, belying how hotly
his breath blasted above her ear. "Does she

shun him or gatherings with friends and family because he has only one hand? I should say not. Not the way he beleaguered me—at her behest—to attend."

Isabella turned her face toward his, and whispered back, "One hand, you say?"

After a brief pause, his body unclenched and he led hers in a sweeping circle. "You didn't know?"

"She never spoke of it."

"You didn't know!" He barked a laugh. "The irony. Just as I did not know you couldn't see—you get along remarkably well, you know, have impressed me from the moment your dangling curl cast out a lure I couldn't resist." He slowed and nuzzled her cheek. "I wish we were alone. I'd show you how very much I have come to adore your defiant ringlets and everything about you."

"But—your heir," she protested weakly, knowing that was the primary purpose of any peer's wife. "We possess no guarantee I could birth your heir or...or that he wouldn't be blind."

"Then we'll love him all the more. *All* our children."

Her heart skipped at the feel of his lips

brushing her temple just beneath the sash, skipped more at the realization he was completely serious. "Nicholas..."

But he had yet to be completely honest with her. He might profess wanting her as wife, but would he ever put his faith in her as he bade her to trust him? Enough to talk of *his* trials?

"I knew Edward was injured," she said, "that it took him a long time to walk without a limp, and I knew his fingers were crushed and broken, but that he can now write again, albeit in a hash per Harriet. And Lord Warrick—the consequences of his injuries are on display, much to his chagrin, I am sure. But yours?" She leaned up on her toes and kissed the skin she found, his jaw, she thought, gathering courage to broach the topic yet again. "You speak of a future with me, but you share naught of your past."

For the first time since he took her into his arms, his feet staggered. Stutted upon hers. "Blast it, forgive me. Your toes—"

"Might sting a few seconds, but that is nothing compared to the pain of your silence."

"Damn me. Did I not claim you saw more clearly than most?" His hands broad across her back and shoulders, he pulled her closer and dipped his head as his feet once again took up the rhythm of the dance. "For years, I trained myself to avoid attachments and evade entanglements—to anyone or anything that might cause *me* pain. But the war blasted that to fritters. Battle itself is wrought with misery. Excitation—and fear for your life—carries you through combat. But afterward? When things quiet? That is when the demons rise up, try to purloin your soul."

Her fingers groped for his, gripping tight once found, as she sought to steady herself against the anguish that met her ears.

"With you, though?" Grit coated his words. "Despite my prior proficiency at shunning soft feelings toward others, from the onset of our acquaintance, there was no avoiding or evading. Only pursuing."

Relief, that he was finally revealing his sweats and struggles with her, gave her lips a saucy tilt. "I noticed the pursuing. But Nicholas..." Her other hand drifted from his waist to that area where her fingertips sensed his heart thumping as riotously as hers. "Those past experiences, whether you want to acknowledge them or not, they still affect you.

And so much of you is hidden from me"—she released his hand to gesture toward her covered eyes—"that I cannot bear the thought of you fighting these demons by yourself."

"I know," he said on a haggard groan that vibrated through her. "I know." His feet slowed. He swallowed hard, then bent his head to nuzzle his lips against her forehead. "Part of me wants to share some of that with you. Most of me wants you to never learn of it."

"I am strong enough to carry those burdens, if you like. Whenever you are ready."

"I begin to realize the veracity of your strength. Before chancing across an enchantress with a defiant curl and stubborn will, I thought avoidance was all I needed to find a modicum of peace. Convinced myself that would suffice." His hands wrapped tightly around her waist, fingers splayed warm and wide across her back in between her shoulder blades. "What I needed—what I *need*—is you."

She bit her lip against the sob that threatened. The pain in his voice, the stark honesty that breathed through it...

Had anyone, ever, needed her? Her blind, blighted self—to hear Father speak of her worth—now mattered more than she ever could have thought. Mattered to the most dearest person she knew. "I love you more than I thought it possible to care for another, you most wonderful of scowling wretches."

"You have a tendency to transverse my scowls till I appear the besotted wretch indeed."

She hugged him harder, fiercer, until she sensed some of that long-held anguish leaving his bunched muscles. "'Tis a hidden talent of mine, you know, one of many you have yet to discover."

"*Yet* to discover? I cannot wait to unearth each and every one." His mouth moved, pressed against hers once, then he straightened. "But that is for later. I am nowhere close to being finished dancing with you. Here now, enjoy yourself tonight. I promise to address and resolve each of your concerns tomor—"

"*What in Hades is the meaning of this?*"

The unmistakable bellow threatened to slay every spark of hope and happiness she'd found.

"Isabella? Where in God's name are— *Dancing?* Redford, how *dare* you condone such a farce!" The musicians screeched to a halt. The sounds of sashes slipping over heads and couples shuffling back did little to mask the seething tirade spewed their way. "I arrive home early to find you gone...then ferret out your whereabouts only to discover you making a mockery of yourself? Flaunting my attempts to disguise your deformity? Ungrateful wretch!"

Isabella swallowed but made no move to extricate herself from Nicholas' embrace. It was the only thing propping her up. "F-father," she stammered then took strength from the man holding her. *Unreasonable* fear, she reminded herself. "Father, did you have a happy Christmas?"

"Isabella!" he roared, and a mile away the goose honked its displeasure at being woken. "Come, girl! We leave for Spierton this instant."

She slid her arm from Nicholas' shoulder and he immediately took her hand between his. "Married?" she whispered. "Are you certain?"

"Aye."

"Come, Isabella!"

Squirrel squitters, had he always sounded so unflinchingly brainsick?

Just as she opened her mouth to refuse to

blindly obey like a whipped dog, Edward's voice broke through the increasing murmurs. "Lord Spier, let us repair to my study, shall we?"

One arm secure across her waist, Nicholas guided her forward. "I believe that's best. We'll conduct—"

"No, god-damn it! What's best is if my daughter removes herself home where she cannot make such a fool of herself—or me. Come, Isabella! Take off that idiotic scarf and get in the coach. Now!"

They'd reached him—the ringing in her ears confirmed it. "Nay."

"What?" His astonishment was clear. "You *dare* defy me? Dare shame me in public?"

"Lord Spier." Nicholas spoke softly but she swore it sounded like *Spider*. Imagining the look on her father's florid complexion at the insult had Isabella biting her cheek to retain her solemn composure. Mayhap that's why he'd done it... Nicholas, her champion of champions. "The only one shaming themself is you. Let us retreat to the study and conclude our business there."

"Who in Hades are you?"

Isabella cringed but Nicholas handled the

introduction with an aplomb that had her smiling despite her bit-upon cheek. "Nicholas Michael Henry Winten, seventh Earl of Frostwood, ninth Viscount Haverleigh. The man who *will* be marrying your daughter. Now do we discuss settlements in front of everyone or in the privacy of Redford's study?"

———————◦◦◦———————

"Can you make anything out?"

At the whispered words, Isabella muffled a shriek and scrambled to her feet. "Anne?"

"Of course it's me, silly." Her friend's voice held laughter. "You're listening *under* the door? What happened to keyholes?"

Isabella's face heated. "These blasted doors are thick."

"Think you I don't know it?" Anne touched her arm and indicated she should follow. "That's why I learned to listen via the chimneys. Let's get you settled in the library. I know Frost will want to speak with you privately. What a grand night this turned out to be!"

"Oh Anne, is it really true?" Isabella chafed one upper arm as they sped through the hallway. Chill bumps pebbled her flesh. "Can it be?"

"True as a tuppence, dearest." The fire crackling in the hearth of the room Anne led her to spread its warmth over every inch of exposed skin the instant they crossed inside. The scents of old books overrode that of the holiday greenery and Isabella inhaled deeply, the smell reminding her of learning and her mother. A sense of calm came over her.

Things would work out now; they had to.

Anne guided Isabella to the leather sofa where both women sat down. "Now listen to what else I learned—your father refused to dower you and Frost fairly snarled in his face, saying Spier's bloody blunt wasn't what he wanted. He refused to accept anything but your hand, vowing to stand in favor of some bill your father's been trying to raise but only if *he* swears to demonstrate absolute support of you in public. It was that or never show his 'puffed-up pompous arse' in London again."

Isabella smiled past her remaining unease. "Pompous arse? Nicholas said that, did he?"

"And much more." Anne leaned sideways and hugged Isabella, taking one hand and placing it upon her belly. "Just think, by our next Christmas celebration, you could be the one *enceinte*."

Isabella's face blazed with the heat of a thousand candles, heat that quickly spread downward. Nicholas' child...in her womb. Easily could she envision such a thing. "Aye, and I have you to thank."

"Pshaw. Think noth—"

"Ladies," Lord Redford spoke from somewhere near the doorway. "Anne, now that your plans have come to fruition and you have proffered felicitations, we still have a great many curious guests to reassure."

"Your plans?" Nicholas exclaimed as Isabella sputtered silently.

Anne jumped up. "Blame Harriet. She put the notion to me the first time she met Frost."

"Harriet?" Isabella found her voice.

"She said you'd not be frightened by his scowl and Frost was surely fierce enough to overrule your father."

"Smart sprite, that Harriet." Her body listed toward his when Nicholas lowered onto the sofa and drew her close. "Now I'm doubly grateful I salvaged her damn—ah, deuced goose. Please tell the scamp she retains my unending gratitude—*after* you see your way to shutting the door behind you."

"Yes, sir!" Edward snapped smartly.

"'Night, Frost. G'night, Issybee!"

The latch clicked. Enshrouded in deafening silence, she turned toward Nicholas. "My father?"

"Won't trouble you further. You have my word."

Not at that knowledge so much as the realization that the man at her side would always be so—a true champion, she'd somehow stumbled in front of—Isabella felt her heart take flight. Her fear too. "I do believe I could levitate, how happy you make me. I should have known if anyone could out order my father, it would be you."

"Well, now that I know what a rotten arse you have been subjected to, I shall do my utmost never to issue another command within your earshot again."

She wanted to graze her fingertips over the shadowed jaw of his face. The masculine stubble Isabella had felt during their kisses a time or two had made her breasts and body burn wildly. She wanted to turn toward his chest and touch him in ways no maiden should ever dream, but she contented herself with snuggling deeper into his embrace. "'Tis all right. From you I have come to feel cherished by them. No one but Mama ever treasured me the way you do. Only *she* never stole kisses."

"Paid with berries, I'll have you know."

The corners of her mouth did levitate then. "They'll be free from here on out."

One finger trailed over her cheek. "Issy-belle, was there no one else to deflect his wrath? No siblings or...anyone?"

She gave a slight shake of her head. "None who lived. After me, Mama carried five more babes. Two were stillborn. The others abandoned her body too soon. You...you don't think that will happen with ours?"

"I do not. Somehow those little babes knew the time and place wasn't right for them. They knew..."

"That my father's a pompous arse?"

She heard a snort of laughter then he sobered. "Issybelle, I begin to think in you I have found my own guardian angel, one who will soar at my side and correct me when needed, one who I cannot wait to share my life and love and the seed from my body with. But now I must address one more item before we proceed into the unending bliss I hope we advance toward with our every breath."

He sounded so very solemn...almost unsure for once. She craved the sight of him, wished with all her heart she knew his countenance and could match inflection with an image. "What concerns you so?"

"You have no doubt heard how very uncaring I am? How even my mistress found me so lacking she gave *me* my *congé*? How my own mother died from despair over never seeing her neglectful, coldhearted bastard of—"

She did touch him then. Rammed her pointy elbow in his side. "Stop it, Nicholas. Whatever people may say, we both know those are untruths."

"Do we?" She imagined the lift of an eyebrow at his flippant tone and wanted to clobber him then.

"I cannot answer as to the mistress part and cannot help but think *that* topic shall be one best left in the past—"

"Forevermore and gladly. Who needs a mistress when they have a goddess in their lap?" He suited action to words, pulling her close and leaning back into the corner nook of the sofa. "In their *life*, one can only pray..."

Ready to assure him he misread nothing, Isabella paused when he tensed beneath her. "But I find I must elucidate for my own peace of mind. May I?"

"Certainly."

"Before I begin, share with me what you have been privy to so I may know the depths of grievances I must account for."

Her heart melted at the seriousness with which he took the accounting she truly didn't require. "Only that of your..." She bit her lip before proceeding, unwilling to wound him with her words. "Forbidding, unfeeling nature, which kept you apart from your mother. That and your propensity to glower."

He blew out a frustrated-sounding breath. "You must understand the woman who delivered me of her loins considered her duty ended there. Nannies saw to my care and I enjoyed the sporadic attention of my papa, but my mother was an unpleasant shrew who criticized everyone and everything around her... with one sole exception. My sister Althea."

"You have a sister! That's—"

"I don't, not...any longer." He spoke so quietly, so gravely, Isabella knew not to interrupt again. Whatever burdens this man had been carrying, they chilled him to his soul. It was time he released them once and forever.

But though she waited patiently, further explanation failed to greet her ears. Finally, after another full minute of silence, Isabella encouraged, "Nicholas? Tell me what happened. I need to know."

As though being given permission freed them, his words flew swiftly then. "Althea personified perfection in our mother's eyes. I adored her as well, which might have been counted a surprise, given the disparity with which we were regarded. My sire confided to me years later that Althea had been conceived on the wrong side of the blanket while he was away." Isabella felt a tug and realized she still held tight to the silk sash; now Nicholas held tight to it as well. "After delivering the requisite son on her first attempt, she banished Papa from her bed...but I digress. Althea was the only living person Mother had any affection for. Actually, it was an unreasonable attachment my mother showed her second born. For Althea did all she could to escape the confining clutches of her governess and Mother, plastering herself to my side any time I was home from school."

His fingers slid up the sash until they intertwined with hers.

"During one such visit, I transferred the cough going round Harrow, and before I knew it, Althea was gone. Mother blamed me and in her grief exiled me from Frostwood. I was eleven at the time and didn't realize how cruel a woman she could be, simply accepted the punishment as my due."

"But what of your father? Why did he not step in and take her to task?"

"*My* father?" Nicholas squeezed her fingers and gave a snort of something that could possibly be taken for laughter. "Because that would have involved exerting himself. He wasn't a bad man, just indifferent most of the time, more interested in fox hunting and ferreting out pheasants than dealing with what he considered petty household squabbles.

"It was easier to relocate himself to his favored hunting lodge and me to school. He told me once, when we were grouse shooting and he'd taken to avoiding his wife by choice, that he thought I was better off not having to listen to Lady Miserable shriek her cutting insults any longer. I think in some ways he may have been right. I'd learned by then it was safer to rely only on myself. Easier that way—no chance of rejection. I refused to allow anyone close save a comrade or two until...you."

Isabella ached for the little boy he'd been. "Nicholas, tell me you realize what happened with your sister was not your fault, none of it."

"I do now, from the vantage point of more years and, alas, more wisdom. It was Christmastime when I last returned home...and played with Althea. Ever since, at the first hint of the season, I shove away the memories, attempt to regard the holidays as nothing... nonexistent. Which, until this year, meant denying memories of Althea as well." As if noticing the intensity with which he spoke, his voice gentled. As did his grip upon her fingers. "With Mother gone, I *wanted* to spend this Christmas at Frostwood Hall but just the merest reminder of the holiday froze me in place. I couldn't fathom going...alone."

"Then we'll go together."

A clock chimed somewhere in the room. "Midnight," he murmured, stroking one hand up her arm. "January 6th, the day of Epiphany...and I do believe I have been blessed with one myself. It wanted your presence, your love." His fingers gripped her shoulder. "*I* wanted your presence and love, did I but know it. That's what was missing before I could return home."

Feeling more secure—in his presence and love—than she would've believed possible a fortnight ago, Isabella vowed, "You have both, my scoundrel. *My* Nicholas..."

He went on to explain how after selling his commission, he resided in London, not having enough fight left in him to challenge his mother and have her bodily removed to the dower house. "My solitary visit to the estate was greeted with a barring of the door and orders, via a lowly footman no less, to never show my face again. After being subjected to bloody battles abroad, I didn't see the need for causing one at home. Which isn't to say I haven't made other attempts at reconciliation for I have, especially since Papa died. Coming into the title I felt a sense of responsibility to put the past to rights. Yet just as they'd been twenty years ago, my letters were rejected—all returned with the seals unbroken. And there you have it, why I'm accounted a horrid son—a combination of her preference and my own stiff-rumpled pride..."

"Pride? Another foible?" Isabella turned in his arms and kissed his whiskered jaw, running her fingertips over his cheek—sans dimples, she couldn't help but discern. "Well, Nicholas Michael...was it Harry? Winten, *I* think you are the very best of men and would have made the very best of sons, had she allowed you."

"Henry," he corrected without inflection. "So you don't think I'm a coldhearted bastard, eh?"

Was he jesting? Or serious? She tapped his chin. "I know a man who goes out at night to stable a goose of all things because he cannot abide the downtrodden look of another is *not* unfeeling. A man who befriends a lonely, blind woman—"

"Now you stop it. How dare you term yourself such?"

For one so smart, he'd fallen into her trap quite nicely. "You just termed yourself a cold bastard, did you not?"

He cuffed her wrist and slid her arm down until her palm sheltered his rapidly beating heart. "Does this feel cold to you?"

"Nay." It was a whisper.

"I'm on fire for you, have been since the moment you declined to dance with me. A common occurrence I'm none too pleased to note."

She flexed her fingers against his chest then crawled them higher to pluck at his neckcloth. Once a fair amount of skin was exposed, she tucked her face into the curve of his neck. "I'll never refuse you again."

"You better not."

"Aye, sir."

"Impudent wench."

"Aye...sir."

The last was sighed and Nicholas, finally feeling the weight of his own guilt lessen, expelled a matching one. That was when he noticed the sash twined within his fingers. On a whim, he lifted the silk to his forehead and knotted the fabric after securing it over his eyes.

Sensing his odd movements, Isabella propped herself up on his chest—or so the dual points of her elbows told him. "May I ask what you're doing?"

"You may indeed." Blindly he reached for her hand and brought it to his face, realizing as he did so how very significant the impulse of a few seconds prior. "Think I'll wear this the remainder of the evening, and again once I get you home to Frostwood Hall."

Her searching fingers discovered the sash. "Whatever for? Have you knocked your noggin askew, you diswitted man?"

"I think it's only fitting I occasionally take the time to view the world as you see it."

As his meaning sank in, so too did her body atop his. "Oh, you wondrous, *wondrous* man."

"Aye, I'm beginning to believe I just might be, thanks to— *Mmm*." Her mouth devoured the rest of his sentence, which was fine with Nicholas.

Only after more words, more cuddling— and many more kisses—did the challenging events of the evening take their toll and sleep overtake her...*his* Issybelle.

Holding her in his arms and against his heart soothed any number of cold, lonely nights he'd endured as a boy. Erased any number of solitary, soused evenings he'd spent wondering why a French cannonball hadn't put an end to his guilt, along with the rest of him.

Cradling this precious woman, feeling the innocent wisps of air as she peacefully exhaled, breathed forgiveness and new life into an old existence and left him smiling deep inside as he too drifted off to snowy dreamland.

———————◦◦———————

"ARE YOU READY, *my child? To say goodbye ere we begin the next stage of our journey?"*

"Am I! I have been waiting ever so long..."

———————◦◦———————

"I HAVE BEEN WAITING EVER SO LONG for the right woman to find him!"

Radiant, a young girl tugged forward the man behind her and presented him as she would a peer to the royal court, curtsying deeply. She rose regally and held out his hand. "I give him to you now and forevermore, Lady Isabella Jane Spier." The child clapped her hands with such abandon, a burst of air wafted forth. "Soon you'll be Isabella Winten, Countess of Frostwood! How splendid is that?"

And in the perplexing, mystifying manner of dreams, Isabella observed herself as she stood and offered a curtsy of her own to the immaculately groomed, breath-stealingly handsome man before her. "Lord Frostwood, I presume?"

How did she know?

"Call him Nicky," cried the child just before she flew off—on wings!

Wings Isabella hadn't noticed before, her interest totally arrested by the man who graced her with a smile brimming with such love and caring—and bracketed by such adorable, *discernible* dimples—had his visage not already stolen her breath, the look in his eyes would've rendered her mute.

Time ceased to advance, giving her all manner of opportunity to absorb every detail of his appearance, which she did, all the way down to the slight droop on one side of his tailored jacket—something in his pocket, perhaps?—then returning upward to marvel at the breadth of his chest...the deep brown fathomless eyes that gazed so intently into her own...the tiny nick marring one eyebrow...the shadow of whiskers framing his jaw...

Highlighting lips she could not wait to feel upon her own. To—

"Isabella?"

"Isabella? Issybelle?" Gingerly, Nicholas shifted the bundle in his arms. "'Tis time to awaken, my love. I hear the house stirring." Through the window, he also saw the fiery orange ball glimmering beyond the barren trees and couldn't believe he'd actually slept through a sunrise. Talk about the season for miracles!

She moaned and nuzzled his neck, making no attempt to move from her sprawled position over his body. Pity he hadn't thought to lock the blasted library door.

Pressing his lips to her temple, he tried to speak sharply but failed, his words sounding every bit the caress they were. "We may be considered betrothed as of last night, but that doesn't give either of us leave to ruin your reputation this morning."

"Does it give us leave to *leave*?" she asked in a sleep-husked voice. "Perhaps you could begin ruining me on the carriage ride down the drive?"

"If you continue tempting me with your warm body and warmer bum"—he lifted his pelvis into her posterior to emphasize his point—"we'll both be ejected from Redford Manor and invited never to return ere we have time for breakfast." That finally reached her, if her sultry giggles were anything to go by.

"How do you do that?" he asked as she slowly straightened and began the task of tidying his neckcloth, which she'd completely unwound some time during the night. "Laugh with the joy of a schoolgirl yet the seductiveness of a siren?"

"Do I now?" Her cheeks flushed bright. "'Tis one of those hidden talents I promised you would discover about me. Much like my dancing."

"A lady of continual mystery, eh?" She still lounged on his lap but more primly than before, if one could call such an intimate position *prim*. He made every attempt to right his own clothing before a servant—or their fine hosts —thought to knock on the door. "Aha—you just called your dancing a talent. So you're ready to claim that gift you have? I'm gratified to hear that as Frostwood Hall's ballroom rivals that of any you can imagine."

"Truly?" Her eyes widened.

"Truly. And I promise to show you where it's located in the rambling mansion I grew up in if you promise me a dance every evening before we retire to bed."

She pursed her lips as if in deep thought. "Well...if you agree to put bells on this," she pulled tight the horrific knot she'd just tied and tucked the ends of his neckcloth inside his shirt, "so I can find you anywhere I please, I could always promise you a dance *in* bed."

"Minx," he laughed.

"Glorious scoundrel."

"You know, you have the look of your mother when you smile." The words burst from him without thought.

"Oh my. That is the highest compliment I could receive. Mama was the most beautiful— Wait...how would—? When did you see her?"

"I don't..." *know*.

But he did—even as he grappled for an explanation a sudden flash of recollection, of recognition solidified in his mind. While he slept, he'd been visited by an angelic spirit of uncommon beauty whose serenity and warmth was unmistakable. He'd known in an instant she was his Isabella's beloved mama. But more than that, the woman had been holding the hand of his sister! Dear Althea as he'd always wanted to remember her—golden curls dancing and impish smile beaming.

Spirits be damned, he thought, *they'll stuff me in Bedlam if I confess to such a thing.*

Is it any different than Warrick's battlefield angels?

"'Tis a bloody miracle," he said as his mind boggled and heart struggled to believe, "but I'd rather not begin our wedded life with you thinking I'm a bedlamite. May we agree to attribute my knowledge to the magic of Christmas?"

"We may indeed." At that moment she grazed her hand up the side of his face until encountering his right eyebrow. "It *is* split," she whispered. "How very wondrous."

"Wondrous? My eyebrow? Now that I think on it, we're two of a kind, are we not, in the blemished-eyebrow arena. But how did you know? Harriet again?"

Isabella recounted the dream she'd woken to, ending with how she *saw* the most handsome man being given into her care. "Another miracle of the season. And if it's any consolation, I shall forever remove *lack of modesty* from your list of foibles. When one looks as you do, only *false* modesty would be considered a failing."

"Ah...not that I'm one to discount the spirit of Christmas and what magic may ensue, but mayhap you only imagined I possess a fair countenance. For which I'm pleased, I assure you."

Her brow furrowed for but a moment. "Your pocket! Your right pocket—what are you carrying in there, pray? More sticky berries?"

With a hitch in his breathing, Nicholas recalled exactly what nestled inside his pocket. His bandaged left palm recalled as well. "I intended to give it to you last night. Had every plan to—but..."

"But my blasted father intervened."

"And never will again," he vowed.

"Well then..." Her excitement was palatable. "If not berries, then what?"

"I was touched by how you admired the Nativity pieces, how you *saw* them with your fingers. I wanted to give you..." He floundered, the precise words distant from his lips.

"My own Nativity?" she asked in confusion.

"Nothing so elaborate." Attempting to maneuver his handmade gift out of the opening —and past the sash he'd stuffed in there earlier—while snuggling his lover-to-be only muddled his tongue further. "'Tis a token of my regard. A trifling *token*? Regard? No...that's not the right of it. 'Tis a representation of... *Representation*? Nay, not that either." He swore. Swore again when the seam of his pocket ripped, but he finally placed the rudimentary carving into her safekeeping. "Blast me. I'm sounding like a puffed-up prig. It's a *symbol*, one that conveys my lo—"

She stopped his ramblings with a hand to his mouth—this time her accuracy was impeccable. Her eyes glittered brightly, her smile so wide he couldn't believe his fortune...that this beautiful, fey creature who'd taught him so much just with her presence would be his helpmeet, his partner throughout life. *The mother of his children.*

"Aye?" he mumbled beneath her fingertips.

Her other hand, he saw, now lay still upon his gift, after an eager exploration to determine its shape. "A heart...you gave me your heart!"

He kissed her fingers and brought her hand down so he could place it atop that very organ. "Aye, and it only took me four attempts to make the thing. Four attempts and it's still skewed to London and back. If I'd had more time—"

"None needed. I love this one." She flipped over the lopsided heart and traced its outline with her thumb then flung herself against his chest. Her arms a vise about his neck, her lips at his ear, she vowed, "It's absolutely perfect. *Perfect*. As are you."

He hauled her body even closer. "Oh aye— foible-ridden Nicky's perfect."

"For me you are."

And he was.

11

THE FESTIVITIES TAKE AN INTIMATE TURN

A FEW WEEKS LATER...

"I LIKE what you have done in here," Nicholas told his new wife when he found her sitting at her dressing table on their first full night at Frostwood Hall.

Her sable hair was brushed to a silky sheen, her hands strangling the handle of a boar's-hair brush so tightly it was a wonder it didn't squeal.

He knew the flush on her cheeks didn't have a damn thing to do with the nip in the air but had everything to do with them spending the night together as husband and wife.

Indeed, the room little resembled the dragon's lair he recalled from childhood, Isabella's belongings giving it a homey atmosphere he would have found inviting any other time.

But not tonight.

He came up behind her and placed his hands on her shoulders, rubbed his thumbs on the delicate skin of her nape. "Like the pictures especially."

Framed miniatures graced a far side of the circular table, one of Althea and one of Isabella's mother, both faces gazing contentedly from the painted portraits.

She tensed beneath his touch and released the hairbrush with a clatter. But the mirror reflected the peaceful smile curving her lips when she stretched one arm to locate then trace the base of each frame. "Lizzie's idea. She told me they'd be watching over me whether I could see them or not."

Lizzie. The maid who had taken such care of his beloved at Redford Manor. After speaking to Ed, Nicholas had enticed her away, even sent her ahead to prepare the rooms and corridors, granting Lizzie authority to direct the other servants in the placement of furniture and anything else she thought might prove helpful in giving Isabella as much freedom as possible. Smart decision, that.

He'd been making a lot of those since meeting his beautiful, nervous-as-hell bride little more than a month ago. "I think she has the right of it. But come now..."

With a touch so gentle it wouldn't break a bubble, he encouraged Isabella to stand and turned her to face him. A fine trembling had taken hold of her limbs. "Well, my lady, are you quite ready to spend your first night in your new home?"

They'd arrived in the wee, dark hours of that morning. Since, he'd given her a tour of the grounds he and Althea had stomped over, so damn relieved when joyful memories bombarded him from around every corner, every tree they'd climbed, every stall in the stable one of them had traipsed across or hidden in. The house had been fully prepared for their arrival, elderly but still faithful servants greeting him like the long, lost son he was, rejoicing in his homecoming in ways that told him he could have returned sooner.

Ah, but Nicholas knew his timing was perfect. As was his lady wife, now staring uncertainly toward the ceiling. "I...ahm..."

She was adorable in her anxiety. But he'd rather she be at ease.

"You...ahm...*what*?" he asked in a coaxing, calm manner at odds with the riotous burden of carnal desires storming his every cell. Now that they were *this close* to that final consummation, it took every ounce of restraint he possessed not to pounce on her like a rabid dog in heat.

When she persisted in finding the ceiling worthy of all her attention, he cupped her elbows and sought to soothe her with the—nearly—platonic touch through the layers of her robe and night rail beneath. "Isa...bel...la?" he sang softly.

Finally she left off gazing overhead and gripped the lapels of the dressing gown he'd donned after his bath moments earlier.

Her fingers moved reflexively, nervously. "I... It's rather chilly in here, isn't it?"

Time to banish her anxious fidgets once and for all. He bent down and swept her into his arms.

"Nicholas!" Her hands fluttered before she fisted one in her lap and curved the other around his nape. "I wasn't expecting that," she said breathlessly. "Do warn me next time."

"Yes, my lady."

She huddled into his warmth. "Oh, but you feel nice. Where...where are we heading? The...ah...bed?"

Smiling broadly, because she was finally against his body where he planned on keeping her for the foreseeable future, Nicholas walked right on past the bed where his mother had slept. He'd have the servants burn it tomorrow. Her picture might hang in the portrait gallery, but he wasn't about to let the rest of her things hang around. Everything else had already been boxed up and shared with his tenants. But that bed had to go.

"My chambers," Nicholas told his wife, carefully reaching beneath her posterior to turn the knob of the connecting door. "My *bed*, where I hope you'll consent to stay and sleep always."

"Oh, I don't know..." She sounded suspiciously cool. "I think I'll have to decide whether it suits me first."

"Minx." He secured the door, locking them into their own romantic haven for two. As romantic as he could make it.

Fruit and cheese and bread resided under domed trays (for later he hoped, *much* later), mulled wine waited in goblets, and the fire had heated the room to perfection. He even had several washcloths at the ready and a basin of warm water waiting near the hearth—for afterward.

He wanted this time to be special for Isabella. As special as she was to him.

When he stood her on her feet, she turned toward the glow, holding her hands out—but still trembling, he saw. "Now this is lovely. All right, I think I'll stay."

"Will you now? But you have yet to test the bed. How can you be certain?"

"What?" she asked overly brightly, swinging toward his voice. "Shall I jump on it? Test how springy it is? See whether I can touch the ceiling and decide if it will suffice?"

He loved her spirit. Her courage. The way she made him laugh.

"I love *you*." The words rumbled from him and he stepped closer. "And I want to love your body. I have been holding back, waiting—" Not anticipating their vows, no matter how tempting, because he'd never do anything to dishonor this precious woman.

"Finally!" She gained her position by patting his lapels then she slid her fingers down until she encountered the tie at his waist. Which she proceeded to knot further in her attempts to undo it. "It's been plagueing me, wondering *when* you were going to do your husbandly duty."

"We only married yesterday"—at Redford Manor, so Anne and Ed, Harriet and her honking goose could be present (he'd yet to figure out the chit's attachment to it)—"and traveled promptly here—"

"Where anticipation has twisted me in knots all dratted day."

Nicholas grinned at the complaint in her voice and helped her with the tie. But she was shuddering now, despite her brave words.

She needed more time to relax. Fortunately, he'd planned for that possibility. "And now you're going to have me. Not yet—" He stopped her when she started to press up against him, smoothed her beautiful hair away from her face while he imprinted the adorably pinkened features in his mind. "This time is all for you."

"I don't understand."

He reached for the blindfold he'd left on

the bed. "Call it my wedding gift to you—*to us*," he reiterated when her brows drew together. "I'm binding a sash over my eyes..." Which he did, floundering a bit when she started to protest. "Nay, let me. My chambers, my choice."

"*Our* chambers," she chided with a light laugh. "Lest you forget."

"Never. And now..." Lowering his arms, he told her, "I'm taking off my dressing gown and dropping it—"

"Not near the fire!"

"No, no, at the foot of the bed—*ow!* Damn. Laced my toe. Damn, da— Pardon. These trunks masquerading as posts are hard as Hades."

She was giggling full-out by the time he'd situated his naked self in the center of the massive canopied bed occupying the lord's chambers. Blast it, how was he to know the piece of insanely huge furniture would feel so very empty without her?

"I'm in the middle of the bed, eager for your company," he told her, having a devil of a time with the sash—it kept slipping down over his ears. He bunched it up and tightened the knot, telling her as he did so, "Now then, if you haven't moved, the bottommost left corner is approximately three paces in front of you."

He expected, now that she knew her orientation, she'd join him any second. "For the rest of the evening, my darling Issybelle, I am your servant to explore and use as you will. Tonight, we each discover the other on equal footing, as it were."

Her giggles had quieted.

The blackness of his vision amplified the howl of wind outside, the slap-bang of a shutter in the distance, and the lack of sound from his wife. But the fire flamed on, crackling and popping merrily, oblivious to his growing concern.

"Are you warm enough?" God knew he was.

She made an affirmative noise in her throat.

But his ears told him she hadn't moved a muscle. "Still nervous?"

"Just a little."

"Take all the time you need," he said soothingly, exhibiting the patience of one expecting to be sainted any moment now. "I'm not going anywhere."

And still he waited.

And waited.

Damn. Now that he was practically spread-eagle, nude as a babe, baring his soul and body as never before, and *beyond* ready for his wife, she was nowhere to be found. And it was dark as hell behind the thick sash.

An odd choking noise came from the foot of the bed.

"Isabella?" Nicholas scrambled to a sitting position. One long tie of the blindfold flopped against his nose. It was tempting to take it off, to see her in the firelight. But he wouldn't.

He'd meant what he said—they'd blindly learn each other's secrets together. Tomorrow morning would be soon enough to behold all her charms in the light. To tell her how lovely she appeared to him, his charming Issybelle.

For now, he just wanted to hold *her*. So where the dickens was she? "Isabella?"

SEXUAL INTERCOURSE. Mating. Tupping. Lovemaking.

Aye, that was the one.

Lovemaking with her new husband.

There were so many words for it and so much she didn't know. Such as *how* to do it.

Oh, Anne had shared the basic fundamentals, but Isabella surmised intimate relations were much like eating raspberry cobbler. No matter how much description one received from others, one never knew how it really tasted until the crumbly, gooey sweetness crossed from a fork into their own mouth.

But how could she think of food when her stomach was a roiling twaddle of spikes and stickers?

She knew nervousness was to be expected.

She knew it would likely sting—but just for a bit.

She knew her comfort surrounding the act would assuredly improve with time.

She also knew she was not—most certainly *not*—supposed to find any of this funny.

But the tickle in her throat, the gurgles of laughter fighting their way up from her neck, the giant smile she tried to stifle by mashing her lips together, they all said otherwise.

"Isabella?" Rustling ensued and she feared he was about to call a halt to the little game he'd instigated. That or possibly stop his thoughtful seduction altogether. "Isabella!"

"I am f-fine," she choked out. "Stay in bed, I beg you."

"You don't sound fine."

"I'm trying not to laugh."

"Eh?" Another of his adorable grunts. He exhaled loudly. "Sweetheart, if you want to laugh, by all means do so. Only please, would you enlighten me as to its cause? I think I could use a chuckle," he finished on a growl. "This evening is not proceeding how I'd planned."

Which somehow struck her as funny, and she did laugh. Finally. It felt good, allowing the pressure that had built up in her chest a way out. "But that's just it, this isn't going how I'd envisioned either. I thought...ah, doing *this* was going to be a solemn, serious occasion and—"

"But we have kissed a fair amount," Nicolas sounded surprisingly conversational, "more than a fair amount I'd say, and you can't claim those were all sober events."

"Nay, but this is different. For I have been eagerly dreading it all day but—"

"*Dreading* it?" The word dropped like a guillotine.

"But eagerly, mind you. Although now all I can do is picture you with a black patch covering one eye and a red scarf wrapped about your head and—"

"A red scarf? An *eyepatch*?"

"Like a pirate," she explained as she approached the bed. "Because you have stolen me away to ravish me and because you treasure me so thoroughly."

"I can be your pirate." The growl was more subdued this time. More thoughtful.

Reaching the thick post at the corner, she paused. "Is this where you stubbed your toe?"

"Where? What?"

"The bedpost."

"Yessss..."

She feared her wild changes of topics were leading him on a merry chase. And she was about to take yet another turn because a fresh scent, one that reminded her of summer sunshine and the picnics of her youth, was causing her to sniff. Then sniff again. "Do I smell..." Raspberries? Nooo. That would be implausible. "Blueberries?"

"And a whole slew of other berries. For later."

Some imp made her ask, "Mistletoe?"

"Hanging from the rafters," he replied instantly. "Hordes of it, far above your head."

Isabella knew how to recognize his clankers by now; he might not spout them as frequently, but she'd learned well the different nuances in his voice. She grazed her palm up the stout wood column, imagining the just-invented kissing boughs dangling above. "Ah, but since I'm no longer charging for my kisses, I suppose we can leave it all up there."

"Thank God." He sounded ever so relieved.

Which only made her smile. "Tell me, my always, always, *always* truthful spouse—"

"Ha! You know me well."

"I do indeed. You're not peeking, are you? At me?"

"Though I'm beyond tempted, I won't." She knew he spoke honestly. "I'm in the dark as much as you, my love."

And that's when she left off being wary of the unknown, berries—fictional and otherwise —and her very own blindfolded pirate showing her the way. "But I'm no longer in the dark, haven't been since that very first kiss you gave me."

"Issy...belle." Within the drawn-out syllables of her name, he infused a wealth of love.

She tested the scope of the bed hangings and found the center of the high mattress between the fabric-draped posts. Propping one knee on the plush surface, she allowed her dressing gown to slide from her shoulders.

Another deep inhale of berry-scented air for courage and she pulled her gossamer nightgown over her head, only a smidgen disappointed he wouldn't be admiring it tonight. "There now. I have just taken off my robe."

"Have you now?" He sounded almost indulgent.

"Aye, and all that was underneath."

"Y-you have?" he sputtered.

"That I have." Her voice had taken on a smoky tone Isabella was amazed came from her mouth. "And I don't feel like laughing anymore either."

"You don't?" It was a husky whisper.

"Not at all. Shall I tell you what I see?"

"God, yes."

Her fingers crept forward until she sensed the heat coming from his body. Circling a few inches around, she made deliberate contact with the skin of his lower legs.

She'd meant to initiate tentative contact, but the rasp of his manly body hairs tossed that intention overboard and her hands clutched at the muscled limbs. A slow, up-and-down slide of her palms sent treacherous tingles racing from her fingers to set up camp somewhere south of her stomach. That scandalous slide also oriented her between his knees and his feet. So now she knew "where" she was. Supposedly.

In truth, she was swimming in such deep waters she was thankful she could count on Nicholas to jump in with her.

Climbing fully onto the mattress, Isabella took hold of his ankles, one in each hand. "I see a beautiful room, full of strong, masculine furnishings. The smoldering fire casts a golden glow over the warm brown tones of the rug and bed hangings." And because she was awfully curious whether or not she'd do better to modify her initial perceptions, she asked in an aside, "Are they by chance, brown—like your eyes?"

"They will be tomorrow."

Smiling deep inside, she moved one hand from his ankle to caress the embroidered silk counterpane beneath his leg. "I see sumptuous bronze bed coverings and beige linen sheets beneath."

"New ones," he assured. "I ordered them from the best linen-draper in London."

"Thoughtful of you. Now do hush, I have a lot to see yet." Her fingers returned to his leg and she swept them upward, hearing his breath hitch and ignoring the quiver the fine hairs on his legs kept causing in her belly. (Or attempting to ignore it, otherwise she'd never be able to keep describing things, to show Nicholas the world he'd given her.) "I see muscular calves and—oh, dear—slightly knobby knees—"

He gave a bark of laughter.

"And, ahmm..." She faltered when she encountered the firm, flexing flesh of his thighs and the smooth, smooth skin above, and to the sides when she stretched her arms higher and around—way around—certain anatomical protrusions—

"I'm afraid you might have missed something there."

As though battling the urge to reverse direction and go back, her fingers dug into the sides of his torso. "Some things we aren't always ready to see," she answered primly.

By the time she renewed her daring sufficiently to continue on and flattened her palms on the corded muscles of his stomach, Isabella

thought perhaps both she and the man she ex-
plored were shaking equally.

What to do next? Reach forward to stroke
his enticing chest or instead pay particular attention to the private, upright beacon of his,
the one that beckoned discovery as much as it
intimidated?

Inexperience made the decision for her.

Slapping her palms together, Isabella in-
terlocked her fingers and withdrew, sitting
back until her posterior came to rest on his
legs. "I see a woman who's lost her courage to
explore," she confessed, more than a little dismayed when she discerned how very damp
her center had become. "And one who fears
she's leaking and may soon abandon ship if
her pirate doesn't hurry and claim—"

Nicholas surged to sitting so fast he almost
knocked her off the bed.

After only a second's groping, he clasped
her shoulders, slid his hands to her waist. He
hauled her to him, dragging her over that pro-
truding part of him and right up his body until
he held her against his strong and comforting
chest.

Lips at her temple, hand splayed on her

spine, he whispered, "So, my lady, you'd like for your ravishment to commence?"

Isabella lengthened her legs along his, petted the broad shoulders beneath her hands and exhaled, flattening her tender breasts as she melted onto his bare skin. "I think... I think..." She feathered her fingers up his neck and jaw to take hold of the blindfold covering his eyes, pulling it off. "I think, rather than be ravaged by a pirate tonight, I just want my husband to make me his."

His fingers flexed on her back, echoing the twitch of his male part against her abdomen.

"Do you now?" he said as silkily as she'd ever heard him.

Before he could kiss her though, Isabella pushed up onto her forearms and blurted, "I *do* still want to play pirate—only not tonight."

Chuckling deeply, Nicholas rolled to his side, bringing her with him. "I'm certain that can be arranged. But for now, let me arrange you..."

He angled one of her legs over his waist, opening her in the most vulnerable way.

Her body contracted in a series of tiny tremors and he paused, hand just below her knee. "Issybelle? You're grimacing. Shall I stop? Or mayhap slow down?"

Telling her face muscles to behave, she scooted one arm between them to toy with the light whorl of hair in the center of his chest. Now that she knew what he looked like, so easily could she envision the slight, concerned scowl furrowing his forehead, the bisected eyebrow lifted in consternation, the serious, half tilt to his lips as he awaited her reply.

She pressed her hand to his heart. "I'm perfect. Please, continue on."

"Ah," his voice and the image in her mind smiled. Dimples appeared. "Just what I wanted to hear." He returned to stroking her leg as he leaned forward and kissed her. First her forehead, both her cheeks, her lips...

The hand rubbing over her leg didn't hurry, didn't rush, but glided over her skin from thigh to knee, venturing toward her waist a time or two, occasionally shifting to brush her breasts...rousing desire and firing need every bit as much as his ever-deepening kisses.

When her pelvis started shifting forward of its own accord, he pulled back and whispered, "You're ready now."

She whimpered her agreement, trusting. Yearning.

With strong, gentle hands, Nicholas guided her to her back and settled himself over her. His weight was divine.

His staff, lying hot and heavy between her thighs, wicked.

And wanted.

So very wanted.

Her hands roved over his back. His lips worshiped at her breasts.

Nicholas positioned his knees between her legs and spread them wide. Then he meandered his fingers down her stomach and delivered lazy, spiraling caresses through her curls.

He was going so slowly, moving against her body with such grace and control. She didn't want to flail against him like a madwoman, had been fighting the urge to slant her pelvis, to encourage him to move faster, farther...

But oh, the sensations he brought forth with his tender touch. A giant wave threatened to cascade through her, only something held it back. As though an invisible dam stopped the tide from flowing freely.

The wet glide of his fingers edging her

open was more intimate than anything she could imagine.

"Uh..." She licked her lips, her mouth so dry and stomach so fluttery, it was a wonder she still possessed a command of English. "Uh..."

Well, perhaps she no longer did.

He stilled his hand and bestowed a fervent kiss to the base of her neck. "Aye?"

"Those *are* your fingers, right?"

"For now."

"Uhm...for how long?"

He shifted and withdrew from her slick core, kissed her lips and assured, "For as long as you like."

"What if I'd like to feel the other?"

He froze. Then kissed her deeper before pulling back to ask against her mouth, "The other?"

Isabella scratched her fingernails over the barely perceptible bristle shading one cheek—thoughtful man, he must've shaved just before coming for her. "The other as in that impossibly long and stiff part of you I have felt through our clothes for weeks now. I—"

She said no more. It wasn't necessary.

Not when Nicholas scooted his body a few

inches down hers and a slight shuffle between her spread thighs brought his fingers back to her sex, this time with a blunt-tipped offering in hand. "Do you feel me, Isabella?" he breathed against the sloping mound of one breast. "I'm holding myself back, keeping the bawdy parts of me in check, but, darling—"

"But I'm sure I want to meet those parts too."

"My bawdy parts? Well then..." He echoed her gasp as something warm and thick, much thicker than his fingers, slid up her cleft then back down. "This is me, knocking at your entrance—"

"Knocking?" She laughed on a moan. "Feels more like nudging—"

His arm jerked between her thighs, bringing the head of his staff ever closer to her inner depths. "Blast it, woman, this is love talk. Not something I have had much practice with, so I'm not any good—"

She reached down and took hold of his wrist. "You're good," she corrected breathlessly, "great, in fact, so—*ah*—" Tugging on his arm and canting her hips, she rubbed herself along his shaft a few more times. Her knees lifted until her feet were flat on the bed, toes curled into the silky counterpane. "So wonderful I—I think the dam is about to burst—"

"The what?"

And then she was bucking wildly against his body as he brought his head to her breast and licked a narrowing circle around her areola until he scaled the summit. He drew the impossibly tight point of her nipple into his mouth and Isabella forgot how to breathe.

All she could do was feel. Feel the tugging on her breast as it traveled through her stomach to her core where the waves were building, cresting...

"I see it," she whispered fervently as sensations streaked through her, illuminating every corner of her darkened past. "See the sun shining on the ocean—" She gasped. "The beautiful, unending ocean. I see us there..." The waves were crashing through her now, growing ever more insistent. "Hand in hand, we are...walking along the shore, cool water beneath our feet, wet sand between our toes..."

The waves pounded her insides, seeking a way out. And as she continued thrusting herself against the stimulating strokes Nicholas delivered, the dam did break, the tight coil of passion reaching a pinnacle on a heartfelt sigh of pure bliss...pure release...

Eventually the frothing waves settled to a gentle, soothing lap.

"Ahhh." Isabella exhaled, so languid and heavy-limbed, it was a wonder she didn't sink through the mattress to the stone floor. "That was..." Remarkable. Stunning. *Fun*.

Aye, fun. But the gentle lapping hadn't stopped.

In truth, the churning had started up again before it ever fully settled. Her stomach tightened. The muscles in her abdomen clenched and quivered, began to ache anew.

Her breasts ached too, feeling heavier, weightier than she could remember. And her chest felt surprisingly chilled. She brought one unsteady hand to the dampened, previously sucked-upon tip to find it puckered into a tight knot. An exposed knot—one not covered by warm lips.

And still the lapping continued on.

Her hips squirmed as her mind swam up from the depths. "Nich...o...las?" Awareness returned with crystalline clarity. She arched forward, her quavering stomach muscles aiding the effort.

"Nicholas!" A tiny wail emerged when Isabella's outstretched fingers encountered his broad shoulders and she determined what he was about.

Horrors!

Wicked, wonderful horrors!

She flopped back onto the bed, even as her hips lifted higher into his mouth. "Oh heavens. A poxed fox on you—you cannot kiss me there!"

Her lower body disagreed, happily, horridly, flailing again of its own accord against his mouth.

After delivering the most astonishingly intimate kiss yet, he lifted his head to ask, "Are you still nervous? Even the tiniest bit?"

Was she? Startled and disconcerted, yes. Nervous? "Nooooo..."

"Pleased?"

"Beyond expectation?" She answered as though it was a question. Then sought to remedy that. "Deliriously so."

His agile tongue licked up one side of her sensitized folds and back down the other. Another shudder tore through her. "Ever been to the beach? Visited the ocean?"

"Ah...nay." Now that was odd. She'd pictured it so very clearly.

His tongue delved around intimate places too wondrously wicked to name. She caught her breasts up in each hand, pinching the hardened peaks the way his teeth had earlier.

"Fascinating," he mused. "Want to go?" And still his naughty kisses continued.

"With you?" She sighed. Naughty or not, everything he did felt sooooo devilishly splendid. "I'll go anywhere."

"That's what I wanted to hear." His voice smiled again and he climbed up her body. "I do believe it's time I took us both to heaven. Hold on, sweetheart, you might see sparks again. I know I shall."

A second's fumbling and his shaft was indeed nudging for entry. Entry her body greedily offered, having an inkling of what was in store.

Once nestled in place, Nicholas pushed inside slowly and Isabella felt new and different muscles shifting to receive him.

"All the way now..." he murmured before pressing deep, pausing at the last remaining resistance to brace his elbows beside her shoulders. He cupped her face within his palms. "I love you, Issybelle. Thank you for bringing me sunshine and hope."

Then he forged inside the rest of the way, his body filling hers so completely she did see stars, even caught a few on the way down when deep into the night, he told her of the constellations spinning outside their window, painted pictures of the beach they'd visit and the life they'd have, romping with their children over Frostwood Hall and beyond.

And through it all—the gentle washing he administered afterward, the repast of bread and wine, the laughing battle fought with berries upon the giant bed, Isabella saw a man who loved her dearly. And always would.

THE END

Note from Larissa

Howdy! I hope you loved reading *A Frosty Christmas Kiss* as much as I did writing it. This has long been Mr. Lyons' favorite book of mine —he keeps saying it should be made into a movie. :-)

For more *Christmas Kisses*, check out Ed and Anne's story, *A Snowlit Christmas Kiss*. And stay tuned for the forthcoming *A Moonlit Christmas Kiss*, to see Lord Warrick woo an un-suspecting governess.

If you enjoy steamy shifters, be sure and check out my *Roaring Rogues Regency Shifters*. And for an emotional roller coaster of a lord bur-dened by a severe stammer finding love, read *Mistress in the Making*.

Thanks for reading!
Larissa Lyons

P.S. If you are so inclined, please take a mo-ment and leave a review. >^..^<

ABOUT ISABELLA'S BLINDNESS

Though the disorder wasn't recognized during Regency England, Isabella exhibits an aggressive form of retinitis pigmentosa, the term assigned to a collection of degenerative eye diseases. It wasn't until the 1850s when a Dutch ophthalmologist coined the name. RP is hereditary and affects one in 3500+ people worldwide. Fortunately for our heroine, she has a thoughtful—and hunky—hero at her side. >^..^<

Interestingly, the popular tavern the men visit for that beefsteak and ale—Offley's—was just down the street from another noteworthy location: No. 10 Henrietta Street. A certain woman lived there during the time of our story—an authoress many have heard of. One Miss Jane Austen.

WORDS, WORDS. WONDERFUL WISE-ARSE WORDS.

Once words make it into our lexicon and dictionaries today, they have usually been in use for several years. How much longer, then, can we suspicion words might have been around in the past before they made it into some sort of formal recordation?

For years, my goal was to only use words documented prior to 1850 in my historical regency romances. But as technology has advanced, so has the resources available to authors.

For several books, I attempted using only words that were around from 1815 and prior. Honestly, it's exhausting—the amount of research each chapter goes through. Words that you would never think are more modern, like *preference*, can really trip up an author who is looking up thousands of words per book.

To that end, I've decided to return to my goal of 1850 or earlier as my target date for words used in my stories.

Part of what prompted this decision is the word sawbones. Which didn't come into documented use until 1837 (thank you Charles Dickens) but fit perfectly with that early scene where we meet Frost on that wretched, wet battlefield in May 1811.

And, in case you're wondering, the phrase *wise ass* dates from either 1955 or 1971— depending upon what modern resource you consult. ;-)

ABOUT LARISSA

HUMOR. HEARTFELT EMOTION. & HUNKS.

A lifelong Texan, Larissa writes steamy regencies, blending heartfelt emotion with doses of laugh-out-loud humor. Her heroes are strong men with a weakness for the right woman.

Avoiding housework one word at a time (thanks in part to her super-helpful herd of cats >^..^<), Larissa adores brownies, James Bond, and her husband. She's been a clown, a tax analyst, and a pig castrator(!) but nothing satisfies quite like seeing the entertaining voices in her head come to life on the page.

Writing around some health challenges and computer limitations, it's a while between releases, but stick with her...she's working on the next one.

Learn more at LarissaLyons.com.

a amazon.com/author/larissalyons

BB bookbub.com/authors/larissa-lyons

g goodreads.com/larissalyons

f facebook.com/AuthorLarissaLyons

O instagram.com/larissa_lyons_author

MORE BANG-UP REGENCIES

Ensnared by Innocence
STEAMY REGENCY SHAPESHIFTER

2022 Maggie Award of Excellence Finalist

Changing into a lion isn't all fur and games.

A Regency lord battles his inner beast while helping an innocent miss, never dreaming how he'll come to care for the chit—nor how being near his world will deliver danger right to her doorstep.

If Darcy had been a shape-shifting lion who thought about frisking—a lot...

Standalone ~ HEA ~ 81,000-word Novel ~
Book 1 - Roaring Rogues Regency Shifters

Note: This love story between two people contains some profanity and a lot of sizzle, including one partial ménage scene that gets rather...growly.

Deceived by Desire
Steamy Regency Shapeshifter

Meet a Shakespeare-quoting shapeshifter who wants nothing to do with love...

Cursed into the form of a lion without nightly sex, Lord Nash Hammond wants only two things—his liquor strong and smooth, and his wenches wild and willing. What he doesn't need is a virgin!

HEA ~ Book 2 – Roaring Rogues Regency Shifters ~ 97,000 words

Reader Advisory: While Deceived by Desire is laugh-out-loud funny in places, it contains a short *vision* of violence and brief references to past

abuse. Beyond that, expect a fun and sexy good time because...

Changing into a lion is all fun and growls —until it isn't.

───────◄●►───────

Mistress in the Making Trilogy

A fun, emotionally satisfying, steamy tale told in three parts: Seductive Silence, Lusty Letters, and Daring Declarations.

Seductive Silence , Part 1
ebook FREE at all retailers

Lord Tremayne has a problem. He stammers like a fool—at least that's what he learned from his father's constant criticism and punishing hand. Daniel now hides his troubles by barley saying anything. But then he goes looking for a new mistress and finds a delightful young woman who makes him, of all people, want to spout poetry. He thought he had a problem before? Avoiding meaningless dinner prattle is nothing compared to the challenge of winning the heart of his new lady lust.

Lusty Letters, Part 2

Thea's fascinating new protector has secrets—several. Hesitant to destroy her newfound circumstances, she stifles her longing to know everything about the powerfully built—and frustratingly quiet—Marquis. But then his naughty notes start to appear, full of humor and wit, and Thea realizes she's about to break the cardinal rule of mistressing—that of falling for her new protector. *Egad.*

Daring Declarations, Part 3

An evening at the opera could prove Lord Tremayne's undoing when he and his lovely new paramour cross paths with his sister and brother-in-law. Introducing one's socially unacceptable strumpet to his stunned family is *never* done. But Daniel does it anyway. And it might just be the best decision he's ever made, for Thea's quickly become much more than a mistress—and it's time he told her so.

Lady Scandal

Sparks—and stockings—fly when an interview for a husband turns into a game of forfeits—played with articles of clothing—a scandalous lady and one handsome rogue learn how very right for each other they are.

Lady Scandal **awarded the Golden Nib!** "I can't praise this book enough. Regency fans, if you like gorgeous wit in with your devilishly superb, well written, sexy reading matter, Lady Scandal should be on your 'Must Read' list." *Natalie, Miz Love & Crew Love's Books*

Top Pick from ARe Café: "[Lady Scandal] is the most flirtatious, sensual, and delectable treat." *Lady Rhyleigh, ARe Café* ~ Selected as a **Recommended Read!**

LARISSA'S COMPLETE BOOKLIST

Historicals by Larissa Lyons

ROARING ROGUES REGENCY SHIFTERS

Ensnared by Innocence

Deceived by Desire

Tamed by Temptation (TBA)

REGENCY CHRISTMAS KISSES

A Snowlit Christmas Kiss

A Frosty Christmas Kiss*

A Moonlit Christmas Kiss (TBA)

*(expanded version of *Miss Isabella Thaws a Frosty Lord*)

MISTRESS IN THE MAKING series (Complete)

Seductive Silence

Lusty Letters

Daring Declarations

Mistress in the Making - Bundle

FUN & SEXY REGENCY ROMANCE
Lady Scandal

Contemporaries by Larissa Lynx

SEXY CONTEMPORARY ROMANCE

Renegade Kisses

Starlight Seduction

SHORT 'N' SUPER STEAMY

A Heart for Adam...& Rick!

Braving Donovan's

No Guts, No 'Gasms

POWER PLAYERS HOCKEY series

*My Two-Stud Stand**

*Her Three Studs**

The Stud Takes a Stand (TBA)

*Her Hockey Studs - print version